A HOME FOR LOVE

THE LONG ROAD HOME
BOOK ELEVEN

KRIS MICHAELS

KMRW LLC

CHAPTER 1

CANCELED.

CANCELED.

DELAYED.

CANCELED.

ALEX THOMPSON FELT his shoulders slump as he watched the status board at the Atlanta airport update. His flight, recently posted as delayed, plunged into the red canceled column. *Perfect.*

He grabbed his backpack and headed to a corner of a nearby gate, moving away from the hoard of people bitching about the cancellations. Pulling his phone from his pocket, he dialed Nail.

"What's up, man?" Nail, his best friend, answered the phone on the first ring.

"Flight's canceled."

"Figured it would be. That freak early November snowstorm that buried us moved east. The lake effect snow over the Great Lakes gives the national weather people a raging hard-on."

Alex snorted at the visual. "Well, at least someone's getting enjoyment out of the snow."

"Right? Are you going back to Benning to wait it out?" Nail asked, referring to the base where the 1st Special Forces Operational Detachment-Delta, or Delta Force, was headquartered. They'd both served with Delta as operators. Nail punched out on a medical retirement about five years ago, which Alex understood all too well. His commander recently handed Alex his walking papers, also a medical retirement. It was a punch in the gut after working so damn hard to rehab his leg.

"Nah, I cleared out of my apartment. I could couch surf with one of the guys, but ... I'll find a corner and wait it out. There's food here. I'll manage." He wanted to be gone and put distance between himself and the Army. He'd fought damn hard to stay in, to rehab his leg, but a training exercise at Benning took him out of the profession.

Nail had a job for him in Rapid City. Alex wasn't a motorcycle mechanic per se, but he could figure it out. His specialty was big rigs, diesel, and hydraulics. His old man had taught him engines at a young age, and he'd started in the Army as a mechanic. Alex rolled his shoulders and changed the subject. "How's Tank?"

"My old man is a tough son of a bitch. Man, let me tell you, that Covid shit is no joke, but it literally saved Tank's ass. The doc said he'd be dead if he hadn't been in the hospital when he had his stroke. He's pissed he isn't making faster progress, but medically, he's doing great, or so the docs say." Nail's old man was the HMFIC, or head mother fucker in charge, of a local motorcycle club and, from all accounts, a badass mother.

"How's the workload?"

"I'm keeping my head above water. Or should I say snow? Thank God it's winter. Of course, that's when everyone brings their bikes in to get upgrades, a new paint job, or fix minor issues. Plus, we have a couple of custom jobs I'm trying to finish, four more in the pipes." Nail sighed. "I'll pick you up whenever you get in. No worries on this end."

"I appreciate that, and thanks again for the job."

"You're doing me a favor. Once Tank gets back to the shop and can turn a wrench, you can put out resumes and shit. Helping us out on such short notice is a godsend."

"Maybe, if I ever get there." Alex glanced out the floor-to-ceiling window. Huge snowflakes floated down from the gray, cloud-covered sky. "Believe it or not, it's snowing here."

"In Atlanta? Holy hell, that'll shut everything down for days." Nail laughed. "Find the USO. They usually have comfortable chairs."

Alex's eyebrows popped up. He hadn't thought about the USO. "Can I still get in? As of yesterday, I'm retired."

"Yep. Just wave that pretty baby blue card at the front desk, and you're golden. It works just like your active-duty ID did."

"All right. I'll let you get back to work." Alex zeroed in on a bookstore across the way and down a bit. Hopefully, he'd find a book and a comfortable chair in the USO and wait out the hard-on-inducing blizzard.

"Hey, Bull, don't stress about the weather. I'm good here for the time being." Nail shortened his operator handle as all the team did. Bullseye was Alex's original handle, but he'd gone by Bull for so long that most of the younger team members didn't know him as anything else.

"I'm not. I just got the itch. I need to get gone and move forward." He needed a plan, needed structure. If the Army gave him two weeks' notice, he would willingly plan for spontaneity in his schedule. Things lately had been far too fluid for his liking. When he deployed on missions, the consistency of training, personnel, and tactics kept his inner schedule fiend fed. Since the accident, he'd been adrift.

"I know the feeling. Call when you're on the plane."

"Will do. See ya." Alex didn't wait for Nail to say anything because the man wouldn't. He never said goodbye—one of the strange quirks that Alex had accepted about his friend.

Thirty-seven dollars later, with a large soda, a Grisham book, and several bags of chips and candy shoved into his backpack, Alex made his way out of security and to the USO. Stepping through the door, he saw the clipboard. A sign-in sheet. He did what any person who'd spent two hours in the military would do. He signed in. At the rank block, he paused. Retired. Damn, that word was hard to write, but he did it. There weren't many people there yet, but he figured the place would fill up quickly as soon as everyone sorted out alternate transportation. Thankfully, he'd already changed his flight on the app. His eyes followed the brightly painted hallway to one of the many shadow boxes. The unit and personal coins told a host of stories, and he'd like to know how the USO had obtained all of them.

"Hi, we've been expecting you."

Alex jerked around and glanced down at the person who'd snuck up on his ass. She had a brilliant smile, and her eyes sparkled with mischief. Or maybe happiness, he wasn't sure which. Her dark brown hair bounced at about shoulder length. It wasn't easy to judge her age, but he thought about mid-forties-ish. She could be older, but he sucked with ages.

"Ah, I think you have the wrong person." Alex

looked over his shoulder. "I'm just looking for a place to chill until I can catch my flight."

"Yes, the snowstorm hobbled up the connections. I'm keeping the USO open tonight for the ones like you who have to reschedule plans. The weather is settling up north, and usually, things defrost in eighteen to twenty-four hours. The weather has a way of messing with our schedules. I don't like that either."

Alex blinked. "Either?" Had he jumped into the middle of a conversation?

She smiled at him again. "Let me show you where you can relax and read that book you bought."

Alex jerked his head to the side. "How did you know I bought …"

"I can see the impression pressed against your backpack." The woman laughed. "My name is Blessing."

Alex frowned. "Blessing?"

"Yes, sir. My mother always said I was her blessing. And my mom was sure I'd be one to others, so she named me that to seal my destiny."

"Seal your destiny?" Alex followed her down the hall.

"Absolutely. Your name is Alexander, right?"

"Ah, yeah …" Alex frowned. How did she know that?

"You signed in." She winked at him like he was in on her conspiracy, only he didn't know what the conspiracy was. He cleared his throat. "I signed in as Alex."

"Alex is short for Alexander, right? Anyway, it means defender of men, which, as Delta Force, I'm sure you did."

"Wait, I didn't say I was with Delta."

"Ah, but you did. You signed in 1SFOD-D—1st Special Forces Operational detachment, Delta. My husband was in the service. I've learned to decipher unit designations very well."

"Oh." What the fuck else was he supposed to say? Delta Force didn't talk about what they did. To anyone, anywhere, or at any time. It was a point of honor. Everyone knew about the SEAL teams, but Delta was still shrouded in gray, and they never boasted about what they did or where they did it. People tried to pick away the shroud surrounding the special operators, but none had pulled back the veil.

"I'll put you back here. I'm expecting several others because of the snaggled flights. There are drinks through there, and the family room and TV room will fill up soon. We have several families who'll need assistance."

"You keep saying we. I don't see anyone else?" Alex's eyes scanned every room. They were alone.

"Ah, the royal sense of the word, I guess. My relief will be here in the morning. Security, both at the airport and the local police, are fantastic about checking on us when we have events like this. The place is secure. There's no need to worry."

"I wasn't worried." But he had been for her. The military was a microcosm of society. A few rotten apples bobbed unseen in the sea of uniforms. Someone usually weeded them out, but not always.

"I thank you for not worrying about me, then." Blessing laughed and sat on the couch as he dropped his backpack by the recliner. "You know, sometimes doing a good deed for someone can put a person on the right path."

Alex glanced at her, stalling out with the sitting-down action. He finally lowered his ass into the chair and cleared his throat. "Blessing, I don't mean to be rude, but I'm not sure what you're talking about."

"You're not rude." She laughed and stood up. "A series of good deeds is in your future, Alexander.

Life has so much in store for you, even if your time in the military is over." Blessing walked away.

"Wait, how did you—"

Blessing turned and walked backward as she spoke, "You wrote retired on the sign-in sheet." She spun around again. "Don't discount people with dreams. Dreamers keep things interesting." She disappeared down the hall.

Alex lifted an eyebrow. That woman was a bubble off center, as in not quite level in the head, but … hell, she was nice enough.

He pulled out his book, a bag of chips, and soda. He rarely ate crap. Airports were his one exception. Something about the constant chaos of the hubs sent his nerves into overdrive. They always had, so he self-medicated with carbs and sugar. It was better than drinking. He'd seen too many lives ruined by addiction to drink more than a beer now and then. And the distance between now and then was a long, long way.

Some time later, he turned a page and looked up. The other rooms in the USO had taken on more people. Several toddlers were playing with their parents in the family room. Several young, enlisted personnel had plopped themselves down in front of the television. He'd been so engrossed in his book that he hadn't noticed the influx.

Blessing's laugh sent his eyes in the hallway's direction. She led a man back toward where he was sitting. The guy had red hair and a close-trimmed beard that matched the auburn hair on his head. He knew that face.

"Alex, this is Ian."

"Sergeant Ridgeway. Been a while."

"Damn, Bull Thompson, right?" Ian extended his hand, and Alex clasped it.

"It's Alex, now. I'm out." Alex tapped his leg. "Training exercise at Benning ended it for me."

"Shit, that stinks, man."

Blessing interrupted. "Well, I can tell I'm not needed here. Don't forget what I said, Ian. The past isn't as tricky as you think. I'll be back shortly."

Alex dropped Ian's hand, and they watched the woman leave, speaking with people as she returned to the front of the facility. Ian turned to him. "She's …"

"Strange?" Alex provided.

"Definitely, but nice, you know?"

"Exactly." Alex sat down and waited for Ian to settle. "Been a couple of years."

"You're Delta. Shared exercises are rare." Ian nodded.

Alex knew that for a fact. He asked, "And you?"

"I stayed with the Rangers until I got out. I'm heading back home now." Ian rubbed his chin and stared down the hallway.

"Problems?" Alex could tell something was on the guy's mind.

"Huh? Oh, no. It's … I could have sworn I saw someone I used to know, but … it couldn't be. One of those déjà vu moments that hit you hard and leave you feeling waxed."

"I've had that happen a couple of times. Usually because of a girl." Alex lifted his eyebrows, and Ian laughed.

"It was a woman I thought I saw."

Alex chuckled and leaned back. "So, where are you heading?"

"California. I got a job lined up. My grandfather is a Vietnam vet, and he's going into rehab at the VA out there. Still kicking it, you know, but he's going to need some help. The job will allow me to check in on him."

"Cool. What kind of job do you have lined up?" Alex made conversation to pass the time. He'd known Ridgeway in passing. They'd done some training together, although they were in different specialties.

"Lighthouse Security Investigations. They recently opened operations on the West Coast. You?"

Alex sighed. "I've been fighting a medical discharge, and until recently, I didn't have any plans. A friend who got out five years ago asked me to come up and help him at his motorcycle shop."

"Mechanic? You were a sniper, weren't you?"

Alex just smiled, not acknowledging what he did. It was ingrained, and Ian took it for what it was. He continued, "I figured you'd be going security. Guardian or Lighthouse." Ian leaned back in the chair.

"Nah, I've got so much hardware in my leg holding things together that going back to my roots—grease and wrenches—is a good call. The doctors warned me about smashing this thing again. I enjoy walking, so I'll go back to being a mechanic. That was my original MOS in the service and what I did before I signed up."

"You like to work on bikes?"

"Never done it before. I usually work on the big

stuff, but how hard could it be? Not much to troubleshoot." Alex chuckled.

Ian laughed. "Does your friend know this?"

"Yeah, man, he does. He and I were a team for three years before he got injured in a fucking convoy attack."

"Well, neither of us has to lose sleep over roadside bombs or choke points again." Ian lifted his foot to the footstool in front of him.

"Ain't that the truth?"

"Dude, give me your number. If you ever change your mind about the job, let me know. I'll put in a good word for you with management." Ian took down his digits and hit send on a text, so Alex also had his number. Then they visited about people they used to know. A couple of them were no longer living, several of them were promoted out of positions, and one or two had been kicked for cause.

Alex tapped Ian's arm and lifted his chin. "Here she comes again." Ian turned to look. Blessing was talking to another man and heading their way. The guy with her threw back his head and laughed at the same time as Blessing.

Alex stood up with Ian as Blessing entered. "Keep your seats, please. This is Danny Donovan.

He's going to be hanging out with you for the time being. Danny is a SEAL. Both Ian and Alex"—she pointed to each of them when she spoke their names as a way of introduction—"have recently left the Army."

Donovan stretched out his hand. "Sorry to hear that. Not that you're leaving the military, but that you chose the Army."

Alex barked out a laugh. "Just like a SEAL."

"Ah, shit. Did I get myself hooked up with a couple of Rangers?"

"A Ranger and a Delta." Ian cocked his head toward Alex.

"Well, that makes your decision easier to swallow." Alex clamped his jaw closed at the open-door invitation for one hell of a comeback about the Navy and swallowing. Donovan held up a hand and laughed. "You can think it, but you can't say it! There *is* a lady present." The three of them broke into belly laughs. The ribbing between the services could be brutal, but it was good-natured for the most part.

"I think you three will be just fine together. Play nice. I'll be back." Once Blessing left them, they settled into the dark brown leather chairs.

Alex played host since he was the first one

ensconced in the place. "Where were you supposed to be going?"

"Northeast Pennsylvania." Donovan rolled his eyes. "Not exactly Hawaii or a tropical paradise, but I have some things to take care of."

"Home on leave?" Ian asked.

"Nah, I'm out. As I said, there are some issues I need to address. What about you?" he asked Ian.

"Heading home to take care of some issues, too. He's heading to work at a motorcycle shop, and he isn't a motorcycle mechanic." Ian chuckled when Donovan laughed.

"Sounds about right. Army intelligence for you. But hey, what fun is life without a challenge, am I right?" Donovan said.

"Amen." Alex lifted his soda and took a swig. The good-natured fun was just that, and he would not take the bait.

"Hey, man, where can I get one of those?"

"Blessing said they were in the kitchen area. Through there and hang a left," Alex answered.

Donavon got up. "Speaking of that woman. She's got some woo-woo shit going on, am I right?"

Ian nodded. "Something different about her, for sure."

"But she's nice," Alex amended, defending the woman. It was his default setting. He stood up for anyone until they proved they didn't deserve his time or attention. It was the way his father had been and the way his father raised him.

"Oh, definitely. A person can be nice and still be different." Donovan snorted and stood up. "I'm grabbing something. You want anything?" he asked Alex.

Alex shook his head and pointed. "Thirty dollars' worth of airport crap in my backpack."

"Ouch. I'll take free any day." Ian stood up. "I'll go look with you."

Alex settled back with his book and had just found his place when Blessing was back. "Hey, Alex. This is Quinn Baldwin and Roan Thatcher."

Alex stood up. "Good to meet you."

"You, too," Thatcher said as he gripped Alex's hand.

"I hate to interrupt, but I saw on the status board that the flight to Dallas you were on has moved from canceled to delayed." Blessing stared at him.

"But I changed my flight."

"Really? Check your app, just to make sure. I'd hate for you to miss your plane. The weather is clear west of here." Blessing put her hand on his forearm.

Alex pulled his phone out of his pocket and frowned. How in the hell ... "I'm still on the plane. The app says they're boarding in thirty minutes." Damn, how did that happen? He *knew* he'd changed the flight. Hadn't he?

"Your bags already checked in?" the man Blessing had introduced earlier, Quinn Baldwin, asked.

Alex nodded and flipped through his apps. "Yes, air tags say they're in B terminal. That's where I'm boarding."

"Good. I'm so happy you won't have to spend the night with us." Blessing smiled and waited for him to grab his backpack. She walked out with him, her arm linked through his. Alex lifted his free hand to Donovan and Ian as he left. He'd text Ian when he made it to South Dakota.

"Seriously, I'm happy for you, Alex. Give spontaneity a chance when you get to South Dakota. I promise you; it will lead to good things."

Alex stopped and turned toward Blessing, cocking his head. "I know I didn't tell you I was going to South Dakota."

"I saw the final destination on the app when

you checked your flight. You better hurry. There could be a line to get through security." Blessing smiled and turned toward a haggard-looking woman with a toddler as she approached. "Welcome to the USO. You look tired. Please come in. I have a quiet corner with your name on it."

Alex let Blessing get on with her work and headed downstairs to get in line at security, which wasn't long because everyone was leaving and not entering the gate area. He made it. After making it through security in record time, he grabbed his phone from the bin where he'd placed it and opened his app to recheck his gate number. *What in the hell?*

Alex turned to look back toward where the USO was located. There was no connecting information on the app. He had to move to the next page for it to show the connecting flight, and he hadn't done that. Donovan had said woo-woo. The term was accurate. A finger-light shiver ran down his spine. Blessing was every inch a woo-woo person and then some. He shook his head and hitched his pack higher on his shoulder. Give spontaneity a chance. Yeah, no. He wasn't built that way.

CHAPTER 2

Alex stood up and stretched. Working on bikes wasn't difficult. Carburetors were carburetors, even if they were smaller and covered in chrome. As he walked toward the break room and the coffeepot, he chuckled. He'd been at the shop in Rapid for about a week. He and Nail had cleared out the backlog, and things had settled into a consistent influx of maintenance he could handle while Nail did the custom jobs. Although, he enjoyed working on the new builds, too. He helped when Nail needed an assist, and he was comfortable troubleshooting the bikes trailered into the shop. No one without a death wish would ride a bike in that weather.

Alex glanced out the window of the break

room. It seemed like the snow hadn't stopped falling since he'd arrived. Gray clouds, snow, wind, and cold. He poured himself a cup of coffee and another for Nail. The man had been in his office since Alex had arrived. Paperwork was his friend's nemesis, but he forced himself to do it before he started the fun work of building bikes. Tank usually did the paperwork and had tried to come in for a few hours a couple of days ago. But it was too strenuous for the guy. It wiped Tank out. Alex hated it for him, but Tank's prognosis was good. The man just needed to give his recovery time.

Alex added cream and sugar to his coffee and left Nail's the way it came out of the pot. Carrying the cups down the hall, he walked into the office and set Nail's cup down on his desk. Then Alex sat and took a sip of his as he waited for Nail to get off the phone. Listening intently to the other person, Nail sighed and rubbed his forehead before looking up at Alex. The pained look on his face was not good. But with a blink, his expression cleared. "Hey, Phil, I might have an idea. Let me call you back." He hung up the phone.

Alex cocked his head and narrowed his eyes. "What?"

Nail chuckled and lifted his coffee cup to his lips. "Ah, the nectar of the gods."

"Enough stalling. What are you getting me involved in?"

Nail leaned back in his big black leather chair. Duct tape kept the arm pads on, and several strips wrapping the side stopped the material from shredding. The damn thing looked a hundred years old and listed about ten degrees to the right. Nail and Tank spared no expense on the bikes they built and repaired. Their shop was state-of-the-art, but the office furniture looked like they'd salvaged it from a dumpster. "You think you know me that well?"

Alex lifted his boot, shoving his ankle over his knee. Nail and he had been through hell and back. Spotter and sniper developed a relationship, and there was an unshakable trust. He could read his partner. He knew him better than he knew any other person on the planet. "I do know you that well."

Nail chuckled. "That was Phil Granger. He's a guy Tank and I know up in Hollister. He runs a garage and a filling station. Still goes out to pump gas for the ladies. Only his chivalry bit him in the ass. He slipped on some black ice and shattered his elbow."

"Ouch, damn." A full-body shiver went down Alex's spine. Fucked up elbows were no joke.

"Well, he has a garage full of big equipment that the ranchers bring to him to fix during the winter. Tractors, semis, balers, you name it, he works on them. The ranchers trust him, and they don't have to haul their equipment down south. Everyone comes out ahead."

Alex lifted both eyebrows. That sounded like heaven. He loved the big equipment. "He has a garage that can handle the pieces that big?"

Nail nodded as he swallowed a sip of coffee. "Built it recently, so he didn't have to go out to the ranches to work on the equipment. Easier on his old bones, he said. Rumor is he got a good-sized settlement from a civil lawsuit he filed against some corporate assholes trying to force him off his land. He invested in his business. But now, he can't work. He's in a cast for at least eight weeks."

"Shit, that's no good. What's your idea?"

"You."

Alex lifted his coffee cup and took a drink. He knew that. But he'd come out there for a reason. "And what about the shop here?"

"You helped me clear up the backlog. Against my advice and the doctors, Tank is going to come in every morning for an hour or so. He can do the paperwork, but I'm taping his ass in this chair." Nail rolled his eyes. "I don't care how upset he gets. If he comes in, he's coming in to do paperwork only. When his doctor and therapist clear him for more, I'll let him tinker in the garage. If I get behind again, I'll shout and steal you for a weekend or two."

"But it took us a full week of eighteen-hour days to clear the backlog from when Tank was sick. Are you sure you can keep up?" Alex wasn't too keen on letting his friend flounder again.

"We were behind before Tank got sick, man. I had Covid for the third time, and he and my mom went on vacation. You dug us out, my friend, but I should be able to keep up. I hope. But as I said, I'll call you if I need to clear things out."

"This guy Phil, is he a good person?"

"The fucking best, man. People up in Hollister are … Hell, how do I explain this town? The community is tight-knit. People watch out for each other like a military unit would, you know? They have a few interesting personalities, but they're the salt-of-the-earth types."

Alex took a drink of his coffee and absorbed the information. "How do you know about these people?"

"Ah, well … After my medical discharge, I got into some serious trouble with prescription drugs. I hated my weakness, you know? Then I got depressed. No, it was more than that." Nail lifted his eyes. "I was in a bad place. Considered maybe swallowing a bullet. More than once."

Alex leaned forward, his heart pounding in his chest. "Fuck, man, why didn't you call? I'd have been here in a second."

Nail nodded. "I know. But when you're in that hole, it's dark and black, and there doesn't seem to be any way out. I kept digging deeper and deeper. Tank knew a doc who worked up in Hollister. Doc Wheeler. We drove our bikes up and back three times a week in the beginning." Nail shook his head. "My old man, he would not give up on me. God, I love that cantankerous old fart." There were unshed tears in Nail's eyes. Fuck, Alex was tearing up, too. They'd been through so much together. Screw it. Alex got up and walked around the desk. He dropped to his knees and hugged his brother. His leg bitched at him, but he didn't give a flying fuck. They held each other in a clinch that didn't end. "Fuck, man, I can't imagine losing you. I wouldn't be able to …"

"Yeah, I know. Same about you, man. It's just that darkness; it sucks you down." Nail thumped him on the back, and Alex let the man go but stayed on his knees by the best friend he'd ever had.

"This doctor helped?"

Nail nodded. "Saved my life. I know he did. Now, get your ass on the other side of the desk before people think we're dating."

Alex chuffed a laugh, letting Nail extinguish the harshness of the emotion with a bit of levity. He moved back to his chair and sat down. "I'm sorry, man. Sorry you got that low, and I'm sorry you had to go through it." Alex swallowed hard. Nail was his best friend, and damn it, he wished he could have shielded the guy from those rough times.

"It sucked, but I'm a better person for it. I'm in a good place, and Tank and I are a lot closer. None of that would have happened if Tank hadn't decided he would fight my fight until I could start swinging again." Nail shook his head. "He carried me for a long time before I could stand on my own. Now, it's my turn to take care of him. Even if the stubborn son of a bitch fights me every step of the way."

"He will." Alex laughed.

"Damn straight. That's Tank." Nail chuckled, too.

"So, that's when you met Phil." Alex leaned back.

Nail smiled and nodded his head. "Dude, he's the biggest gossip in town. He knows everything about everyone. Kind of like command central. You want to know what's up, you go to Phil. But he, his wife Sarah, and their girls are great people. When Phil figured out Tank had nothing to do when I was talking with the doctor, he pulled the old man over to the garage. Tank ended up elbow-deep in equipment he did not know how to fix. But he and Phil became tight. We ate lunch at the garage or at the diner before we headed back down south. Tank still goes up just to have lunch every now and again." Nail sipped his coffee. "You game for helping a friend of the family?"

Alex sighed and looked out the window. "I don't have a vehicle yet. I sold my truck to Hanger. The manual clutch and my leg did not get along." Alex was building his fences. No, he didn't want to leave the little routine he'd developed at the shop.

He didn't want to make a change. He came there to help Nail. The reasons started spinning in his mind.

"I remember you said that. Look, I have a beater. She's got a good engine and will probably fall apart from rust before she stops running. You can use that until you find one you want. Or hell, until you relocate. Not that I'm looking forward to that." Nail gave him a smirk. "South Dakota is a developed taste for some people."

Alex snorted and asked, "Can you develop a taste for cold, gray, and depressing?"

"Yeah. You really can." Nail laughed. "Are you up for this? I know you don't like surprises."

"Right." His mind whirled with all the reasons he shouldn't and then flashed back to Blessing at the Atlanta airport, telling him to be spontaneous. Well, if that shit wasn't spontaneous, he had no idea what was. "Okay. I'll go up and meet this guy, see the setup. If it looks like a disaster, I'll decline, but if he has the equipment, I'd need to do a good job … I'll do the work."

"We'll drive up on Saturday." Nail extended his hand. "That'll give you time to clear out the rest of those bikes in our bay and wrap your head around what you just agreed to do."

Alex snorted and stood up. Nail got him. He knew Alex would lose sleep over the decision because that was how Alex was wired. On the way out the door, he tossed over his shoulder, "Admit it, you only love me for my wrench-turning ability."

Nail called after him, "One of the many reasons, my friend. One of the many reasons."

*** * * ***

NAIL TURNED the vehicle off the highway, and Alex scanned the little ... village ... because it wasn't big enough to be considered a town. *Was it?* "You drove this far three times a week?"

"At first, it was hard. But the trip back home was short, man. My mind was so full of shit that Doc Wheeler and I discussed. It seemed to be over in a heartbeat. Tank never complained. He shut down the shop, got on his bike, and drove up with me."

"Hell of a drive." Alex hadn't seen a car except for one deputy sheriff just outside Belle Fourche. "No traffic."

"People stay inside when it's this cold," Nail agreed and pulled up in front of a gas station.

There was an enormous building behind it. New, painted gray with two massive doors. Nail put the truck into Park, and they got out.

The door to the garage opened, and a man moved sideways through the entrance. The cast on his arm was propped at an angle by a foam wedge that would make it impossible to fit through any other way. "Phil. Love the new look." Nail extended his hand. Phil shook it with his left.

"I don't," the man grumped. "I had to cut off the arm of my coat and use tape to shut the damn thing." The man turned so they could see the duct tape holding together the jacket at the seam.

Alex chuckled. "Sorry, man."

"You must be Alex." Phil extended his left hand. "Sorry, I can't shake your hand properly."

"No worries." Alex shook the offered hand. He nodded to the building behind the gas station. "Big bays."

"My pride and joy. Come around." Phil led them to the entrance and opened the door. He switched on the lights, and Alex smiled.

"Nice."

"Right?" Phil walked in. "I had it constructed with hurricane tie-down straps. I'm tired of replacing roofs because of tornados. If the whole damn building gets destroyed, that's one thing, but I'm too damn old to replace a metal roof."

Alex rolled his head toward Nail. "Tornados?"

His friend laughed. "They happen." Nail thumped him on the shoulder. "Phil, show Alex your operation, will you?"

"Love to. Over here is a tractor that one of our ranchers is having problems with. The hydraulics are coming uncoupled. He's put new ends on the hoses, but they're still dropping the connection. It doesn't happen as often when the engine and oil are warm, but it happens."

Alex maneuvered himself into position so he could see the issue. "Seems to me he only did half the job. I'd change the connector on the outlets, too. Of course, that means getting *to* the outlets." Alex scooted out of the position he was in. His leg complained, but he was used to the twinges when he extended too far.

A smile spread slowly across Phil's face. "Exactly. Over here is a more modern issue. The ECU is showing a fault code indicating the rail pressure drops too low."

"Do you have a diagnostic scanner and fault code reader?" Alex asked.

Phil nodded toward the wall. "In the cabinet."

Alex walked over and grabbed the handheld reader and the cables from the shelf. He lifted into the cab of the tractor, turned the key to the ready mode, and plugged in the diagnostic socket. "I'm not getting that code, but the DTC is pinging with three different codes, all centered on the electronics, not the rail. I'd start with a software upgrade and then re-evaluate."

Alex turned the key to Off, unplugged the reader, and carefully lowered it to the ground. Phil's smile was stupid wide. "You're hired."

Alex laughed. "Was I auditioning?"

"Yep, and you passed. I can't work for seven more weeks. Realistically, it's probably going to be longer than that. That's the soonest I can get out of this cast. I'll make you a deal. You take fifty percent of the income after expenses while you're working. I need to keep my family looked after, but I want to be fair. I won't be turning a wrench, but I can do intake and keep the schedule. My wife handles all the invoicing. We'll show you the books to keep it on the up and up."

Alex shook his head. "I can't do that."

Phil deflated in front of his eyes. "I can't go higher."

"No, you misunderstood. I can't take fifty

percent. I'll take twenty-five percent. I get a medical retirement. My leg has been rebuilt and has more metal in it than this old boy." Alex tapped the tire of the tractor he was just working on.

"But that's not fair to you." Phil's brow furrowed. "I don't want to take advantage of you."

"From what I hear, you're a fair man, Phil. I don't want to take advantage of you, either. I'll need a place to stay."

"That's the problem. We don't have any room at the house. My niece is coming to stay with us. All the rentals I know of are full or spoken for. You'd be welcome to stay here. I can find a cot for you. There's a bathroom. No shower, though." Phil scratched his chin. "I'd understand if you didn't want to live under these conditions."

Alex snorted. "Phil, Nail and I have lived under some pretty damn austere conditions. This is akin to the Taj Mahal for us. If you can get me a bed, I'll bring up the rest."

"Who's Nail? What do you mean, the rest?" Phil asked.

"He's Nail." Alex pointed to his friend.

"And he's Bull." Nail smiled.

"Ah, a military thing." Phil chuckled. "Okay, but what do you mean, the rest?"

Alex shrugged. "Coffeepot, laptop, books, and a microwave for food."

"Coffee is free at the diner and better than you could make here, but I get your point." Phil nodded and extended his left hand. "I'll get that agreement put on paper. Business is business, and I want both of us protected. I got nothing against a gentleman's handshake, but you don't know me, and I don't know you."

"Sounds good to me." Alex nodded in agreement.

Nail glanced at his watch. "Let's grab a drink at the Spur. Will that give you enough time to do up the paperwork?"

"Probably not. I'm typing with one hand, which means one finger. Can I email the document to you tonight? Brian, you can forward it to Alex." Phil walked with them to the door of the garage.

"That works for me. When do you need me to start?"

"When you can get here. The sooner, the better." Phil nodded back to the equipment in the bays. "There are people waiting to get their stuff taken care of, and I don't want them pulling it from me and taking it down south."

Alex looked at Nail, who cocked his head. "I'll be back up tomorrow with the signed paperwork."

"That sounds great. Sarah will put an extra plate on the table for Sunday dinner."

Alex didn't know quite how to get out of that invitation without sounding like a jerk. Most people didn't have his dependency on routines. His father had always told him sticking to the schedule was important. He'd been raised never to deviate unless it was absolutely necessary. It was how his dad managed the house for the two of them and how he ran his shop. Alex swallowed the immediate objection that the suddenness of the invitation brought to his lips. Instead, he dipped his head and said, "Thank you."

They left and jumped back into the cold truck. "Crank this baby, would you?" Alex rubbed his hands together.

"On it." Nail turned over the engine. "I was serious about that drink. We need to toast your civilian status. We've worked night and day to get the shop through the backlog."

"I could use a soda," Alex said and shivered. "I wonder if they serve it hot?"

"No, but the Spur always has a crock pot full of hot cider going."

"Hot cider?" Alex asked as Nail backed into the street and headed out of town.

"Yeah. They put cinnamon, oranges, lemons, and some other spices in it. Serve it hot. Damn, it's so good."

"No alcohol, right?"

"No. You can ask for the leaded version, but most everyone just gets a coffee cup full of the stuff. Besides, I don't drink anymore. Best not to have a gateway, you know?" Nail drove across the highway and turned into a snow-covered parking area by a new building.

"Nice," Alex said, admiring it.

"They rebuilt it about the same time Phil put that recent addition on the back of the gas station. Both are still shiny and new. A fire took this one out, but they added a place in the back for community barbeques and a hall for receptions and such. It's still connected to the bar, but people don't have to go *through* the bar to get to that side. Pretty cool."

Alex glanced toward the back of the building before Nail turned off the engine, and they hot-footed it into the bar.

A big blond guy behind the bar turned and

smiled. "Well, hell, been a hot minute. How are you doing, Brian?"

Nail stamped off the snow from his boots and headed toward the bar. "Not bad, Declan. How are you?"

"Can't complain. What brings you up here today?"

"My friend Alex here is going to help Phil out until he can turn a wrench again. Alex Thompson, this is Declan Howard. The owner of the Bit and Spur."

"Nice to meet you." Declan slapped his bar towel over his shoulder and offered Alex his hand. Alex shook it and sat down beside Nail. "Sorry that you're going to have to deal with Phil all day, every day, though." Declan laughed and held up a hand at Alex's shocked expression. "Joking. Phil is a great guy and a friend. What can I get for you guys? Coffee is fresh."

Alex relaxed when Declan explained his joke. "I hear you have some hot cider?"

"That I do. My wife makes it fresh every morning. Two?" He looked at Nail.

"Yes, please," Nail agreed.

"Brian? Dude, it's so weird to hear someone call

you that," Alex said under his breath when Declan headed to the back wall.

"Meh, Tank introduced me as Brian when we first came up. I don't care, but let me tell you, it took a hot minute to get used to. You know what I mean."

"I do." He'd been called Bull for so long that he didn't respond when people called him Alex.

"Here you go, gents. I'm going to head into the back for a minute. I have some calls to make. Help yourself to a refill if you want one before I get back."

"Will do," Nail said as he lifted the cup.

Alex did the same. "Smells good."

Nail took a sip and closed his eyes. "Tastes better."

Alex took a sip and immediately agreed. It tasted like winter but warmed him from the inside out.

The door opened again, and both he and Nail looked over their shoulders. Alex took a double-take, and Nail inhaled sharply. "Is that …?" Nail said to him.

"Fuck, it can't be." Alex turned on his stool and stared at the door. "That's a fucking ghost."

The man they were staring at looked up from

stamping the snow off his boots. He cocked his head and squinted at them. "What in the hell are the chances of seeing you two newbs again?"

Alex stood up and crossed his arms over his chest. "I'd say slim to none since you're dead, sir."

Nail kept his seat, but Alex could tell the man was poised and ready to react. The man shook his head. "Meh, that was a mess up on the brass's part. This is Isaac Cooper. Isaac, these two screw-ups are about the best team the Army ever pushed through the sniper course."

"Damn, I bet that hurt, sir." Nail laughed.

"More than you'll ever know, kid." Their instructor, Sergeant William Robinson, headed in their direction. All the reports in the field were that he'd died. Shit, he and Nail had driven by the area where he was killed more than once. "Call me Billy. That sir shit ended for me a long time ago. What are you two doing up here?"

"Bull is working for Phil while he's down. I'm his ride."

"How do you know Phil Granger?" Isaac sat down and looked around. "Where's Declan?"

Alex answered, "He's in the back making some phone calls."

"Oh." Isaac got up and walked behind the bar.

He took down two cups and scooped cider into both. "You want a snack?" Isaac looked at Billy.

"Dude, we just finished eating." Billy shook his head.

"Your point?" the man said and grabbed a bowl, scooping mixed nuts into it. He balanced all three items precariously but made it to the front of the bar. He placed Billy's cup in front of him before taking his drink and bowl of nuts to his seat. Isaac sat down beside Billy. "You were telling me how you know Phil?" He leaned forward and looked at Nail and Alex.

Alex pointed a finger in Nail's direction. "Introduced by him."

"I met him when I was up here working with Dr. Wheeler." Nail shrugged.

"Oh. Cool," Isaac said and tossed a handful of mixed nuts into his mouth.

"So, you'll be living up here?" Billy lifted his cider to his lips.

"Camping is more like it." Nail snorted. "There's nothing to rent around here, so Phil is going to dig up a cot. Alex will sleep in the garage until something opens up."

Billy and Isaac exchanged a look, and Isaac shrugged. "I can ask." He got up and went to the back of the bar, pulling his phone out as he went.

Billy turned to them. "You two still keeping up the skills?"

Nail shook his head. "Moved on."

Alex gave a sad chuckle. "I didn't want to, but I shattered my leg in a training exercise at Benning. I can't move the way I need to. Fought getting out like a bulldog latched onto a raw steak, but in the end, they handed me my papers and told me to pound sand."

Billy shook his head slowly. "Sorry to hear that."

"What about you?" Alex asked.

"I still maintain my proficiency." The guy shrugged. "Doing the classroom thing."

"Up here in South Dakota?" Alex's voice rose a bit.

Billy laughed. "People train in surprising places. It's a nice place with good people, and I work for the good guys now."

Nail leaned forward so he could see Billy. "You say that like you didn't before."

Billy shrugged. "Ended up in a tough spot and had friends who gave me a hand up and out."

"I know that feeling," Alex said. Nail had

offered him a way to move forward. He'd had no idea what to do before the job offer.

"So do I," Nail said. "Alex came out after his discharge and helped my old man and me get our shop in order. Now, he's helping Phil out."

"Look at you, newb. Doing me proud." Billy laughed when Alex rolled his eyes.

Isaac came back. "Boss says we can let go of one of the cabins."

"Newb, it's your lucky day." Billy slapped Alex's back just as he was about to take a sip. The cider sloshed but stayed mainly in the cup.

Alex held out the cup and shook off his hand. "Yeah, how's that?" He was about over being called newb. Sergeant First Class was his retired rank, thank you very much.

"There's a cabin our boss won't need anytime soon. It's about a quarter mile from the gas station, due east. You'll see them in a semi-circle if you follow the road through town. Two small bedrooms, kitchen, furnished, with television and internet." Isaac grabbed another handful of nuts and tossed them into his mouth.

"Wow. Thanks." Alex frowned. "What's the rent?"

"None. Just pay it forward someday," Isaac said

through the tumble of mixed nuts he was chewing. "Unit four. Key is under the fake rock at the front door. Internet password is on the bottom of the living room lamp. Chief wants us back, Billy. There's a meeting in two hours."

"I'm going to the store first." Billy chugged his cider and went for his wallet.

Alex held out his hand. "Dude, I got this. Will you thank your boss for me?"

"Roger that," Billy said. "Come on, Isaac. You can get more food at the general store."

"And you say I have an issue with food? You're the one who wants to stop there all the time. You're losing your girlish figure." Isaac tossed the last of the nuts from the bowl into his hand.

"If you don't shut up, I'm telling Lyric you want to go back on a vegan diet." Billy laughed and headed for the door when the bigger man let out a string of cuss words that could singe Satan's short hairs.

"See you two later," Billy called as he went through the door.

"They said he died," Nail said as the door closed behind the two men.

"Who are they?" Alex replied and turned to

look at his friend. "And who trains people way out here?"

Nail shrugged. "The good guys?"

Alex snorted. "God, I hope so."

"I'm kind of amazed you're taking this so well." Nail chuckled. "You've changed."

Alex shook his head. "No, I really haven't. All this flux is killing me … but this woman gave me some advice."

"Woman, huh?" Nail lifted his eyebrows a couple of times.

"Nah, not like that. She was in charge of the USO. Blessing, that was her name, told me that spontaneity would lead to good things. She had a distinctive personality."

"How so?"

Alex laughed and drained his cider. "Dude, she was kind of witchy. You know woo-woo-ish."

Nail threw back his head and laughed, and Alex didn't blame him. If anyone had told him that same thing, he'd have laughed like a loon.

CHAPTER 3

Kayla Bryce pulled up in front of her Uncle Phil's garage a day early. It was bitterly cold outside, so she hurried to the front door. Someone had locked it. Frowning, she made her way to the back bays. During her mother's hospice care, Phil had told her about the new building in the back. They'd spent over a week talking quietly while her mom's body closed down and failed. Her Uncle Phil had been her rock during that time, and after settling all of her mom's affairs, she'd agreed to come up for a visit. Well, she was here, and she was early. Surprise!

Kayla opened the door and closed it quietly. Then she took off her gloves, shoved them in her pocket, and cupped her warm hands over her ears.

Pulling her hair up into a ponytail was a mistake. Dang, it was cold.

She glanced around and lowered her hands. There was a radio playing in the rear of the massive structure. Strange. She didn't think Uncle Phil was a fan of modern music, but Lady G was singing loud and clear. She wiped her tennis shoes on the mat at the door and headed to the back. She saw her uncle's feet sticking out from underneath a massive … well, tractor-ish thingy. The tan overalls he always wore were dotted with grease. The smell of machine oil would always be permanently entwined with her memories of her uncle. She smiled. A bit of impishness lit up her thoughts. Should she? Why not?

She made her way to where she could grab his leg and then reached down and pulled.

"Son of a fucking bitch!" The roar of a male's voice came from under the truck.

"Oh, no!" Her hands flew to her mouth, and she ducked down, looking under the truck. "You're not Uncle Phil. Oh my God! You're bleeding!"

"You think?" The man held his head with one hand and used the other to move the cart he was on from under the vehicle. Oh, definitely not her uncle. The guy's dark hair and complexion were exactly the opposite of her uncle's dishwater blond hair and light blue eyes.

"I'm so sorry." She popped up and ran toward the workbench, grabbing a roll of paper towels. Then she sprinted back toward the man. Kayla tried to put on the brakes, but her wet shoes slid on the painted surface, and her feet went out in front of her. She landed on her ass with a jolt.

The man was up and over her in a second, blood dripping down his face from the cut at his hairline. He bent at the waist and touched her shoulder. "Are you all right?"

She held up the paper towels that she'd kept in her hand. "My pride hurts, but ... here."

He took the towels and ripped off one, dropping the rest as he mopped his face and then looked down at her with the bright red bloody towel held over his cut. "You fell hard. Are you sure you're okay?"

Kayla rolled her eyes. "I really didn't need you to witness that. I prefer to perform all my graceless moves when I'm alone."

The man winced and shifted his weight onto his other foot. "What possessed you to tug on my leg like that?" As he stared at her, his dark brown eyes seemed to look into her soul. Kayla opened her mouth to speak, but there were no words other than ... handsome, gorgeous, sexy, wow ... and those would not spill from her mouth. Not now, not ever.

"Are you sure you're okay?" He dropped his hand from his forehead to reach out to her. The cut started to seep again.

"I am. I'm okay. You're still bleeding."

"Kayla?" Phil's voice called from the front of the building.

"Back here!" the man yelled back.

He helped her up to her feet.

"What the hell happened to you, Alex?" Phil asked as he made his way around the tractor.

"I think I happened. And what's with the cast?" She pointed at her uncle's arm.

Alex put the towel back against his forehead. "I'm going to go get cleaned up."

Kayla stopped him. "I think you need stitches."

"Nah, I've got superglue."

"What?" both Phil and she said at the same time.

"I'm fine." He waved them off and headed toward a small door, which she assumed was the bathroom.

"How ... what ..."

"I got here early, and I thought he was you. I tugged on his leg, thinking the little trolley you always use would bring you out from under that."

"Which leg?" Phil asked her as she picked up the roll of paper towels.

"What?"

"Which leg did you tug on?"

Kayla looked at the trolley and moved her hands, picturing how he was lying. "Left. Why?"

Phil grimaced. "That's his bad leg. He's got a ton of hardware holding the thing together."

"Ah, crud! You've got to be kidding me. Seriously?" Kayla slapped her head and looked at her uncle. "How am I ever going to talk to that guy again?"

"With words, I'd imagine." Uncle Phil chuckled.

"Stop trying to make me feel better. What happened to you?"

"I broke my elbow. Slipped on some ice. Stupid. I didn't salt the outside as I should have. Alex has been here for about two weeks helping out."

"We didn't get around to introductions."

"I'll take care of that after we get him mopped and stitched up." Uncle Phil sighed. "I'm going to pop over to the clinic and see if anyone can look at that cut. Can you go see if he needs anything?"

"Sure." Did she want to? No. She'd already made one heck of an impression and dented the guy's head in the process. But, because she'd caused the damage, she needed to take responsibility.

She headed over to the bathroom and knocked on the door. "Just a minute." The door opened, and she gasped. "It's bleeding worse."

"Yeah, I had to clean it out. There was grease in the cut." Alex held the blood-soaked paper towel to his forehead.

"Uncle Phil went to the clinic to see if anyone was around to stitch you up." She grimaced and grabbed some paper towels from the dispenser by the sink. "You need to change out that paper towel."

"No, if I pull it away, it'll start bleeding again." Alex moved out of the bathroom. "I don't need stitches."

"Are you a doctor *and* a mechanic?" Kayla followed him out into the bay.

"No, but believe me, this is nothing." The guy snorted and walked away. She could see a slight limp.

"Hey, I'm sorry, by the way. I was a day early getting here and thought I'd surprise my uncle."

She smiled hesitantly when he shot her a glance. "I guess I surprised you instead. I'm so sorry."

"No big deal." Alex moved over to the workbench, still holding the soaked paper towel to his cut.

"I'm Kayla, by the way. I'll be staying with Uncle Phil and Aunt Sarah for a while." A twinge of sadness passed over her. There was nothing in Utah for her any longer.

Alex put a screwdriver back in the holder it had come from and stared at her. His eyes narrowed. Man, when he wasn't bleeding like a fire hose, he was really handsome. His dark hair, eyes, and complexion were fascinating, and those lashes. She'd kill for long lashes like that.

He shrugged. "When he said niece, I thought you'd be his daughter's age."

Kayla laughed. "No, my mom was fifteen years older than Uncle Phil. As she liked to say, he was a big surprise for Grandma and Grandpa. Mom grew up here in Hollister, but when she and Dad got married, he was in the Air Force. They retired in Utah, and we never came back."

The door opened, and both turned toward it.

"Back here," Kayla called.

"I don't need a doctor." Alex rolled his eyes and winced a bit.

Kayla pleaded, "Humor me on this, okay?"

He looked over at her. "I don't know you well enough to humor you."

Kayla blinked at the comment. "Well, that's true, but you will. I'm staying here, and I'm helping Uncle Phil since he seems to be incapacitated at the moment."

Alex snorted. "Please tell me you're not a mechanic."

Kayla laughed as Uncle Phil and another man approached. "Not even close. Seamstress to pay the bills, but I'm not sure what I'll be doing in the future. The world is an oyster, you know. It's exciting not to have any plans and just wing it."

The man's eyes widened, and his mouth opened to say something. "Kayla, this is Dr. Johnson. Doc, this is my niece Kayla, and this is Alex." They both turned toward the men.

Doc Johnson smiled. "I met Alex at the diner when he first arrived in Hollister."

Alex nodded. "Doc."

"Let me see what we have going on here." He looked around. "Kayla, can you find a stool or a chair?"

"Against the back wall," Phil said at almost the same time as Alex.

Kayla sprinted to the back of the big maintenance bay and retrieved a stool that had seen better days. She carried it forward, and Alex sat down. "I don't need stitches." Obviously, the persistent grump in his voice wasn't just for her. But even the growliness was attractive. Dang, she'd nearly knocked out the most handsome man she'd ever met.

"Probably not. Head wounds bleed like crazy, but since I'm here, let me check." Doc Johnson snapped on some gloves and carefully removed the paper towel. He used sterile gauze to stem the seeping blood. "Well, you're laid open pretty good. I think you need five or ten stitches." The doctor shined a light in Alex's eyes, and Kayla winced at the violent jerk of Alex's head. The doctor did a couple more tests. "Well, I think you have yourself a concussion. Your eyes aren't reacting the way I'd like them to. Time to take a trip across the street."

"Mandatory?" Alex asked.

"That's my professional recommendation." The doctor placed the gauze pad back on the wound. "Let's go across the street, and I'll have you stitched up in no time."

"I don't have insurance, Doc. I'll need to pay you in cash."

"I have insurance," Phil said. "You're covered under the garage. Go get this taken care of, Zeke. It happened at work, so it's covered."

Alex nodded and headed toward the door. The men stopped, and Doc helped Alex get into his jacket while he held the gauze in place.

Kayla sighed and plopped down onto the old stool. "So, that was fun. He hates me."

Phil chuckled, and she gasped when he turned. "What did you do to your coat?"

"I had to cut it to get it on. Sarah helped me into it, but I couldn't fasten the front, and I about froze. So, when I got here, I cut off the sleeve and opened the side. I can flap it over and hold it with duct tape. At least my core is warm that way."

"Oh, Uncle Phil, this is a disaster." She examined what he'd done. "I can fix it. I have my sewing machine in the car, and I think I have a zipper long enough, too." At least he'd cut the fabric at the seam. She hopped off the stool and looked under his arm. "Did you keep the sleeve?"

"Sure, I shoved it in my desk drawer up front, but I can't use it."

"Yes, you can if I add snaps. I'll cut the seam of

the arm and add buttons and loops so you can wrap it around the cast. I think snaps around the opening here." She traced the armhole opening. "And I'll add a bit of material under the arm. Isn't it cold in that cast without something over it?"

"Freezing," Phil admitted.

"I can fix it now." She nodded and started out to her car.

"Kayla, why are you a day early?"

She stopped and turned back to look at her uncle. "I finished everything I needed to complete for Mom's estate, and my application for the design academy came back. I didn't get in."

"Did they give a reason?"

She nodded. "My designs weren't innovative or interesting. Low-end market and rudimentary was what one judge said. It was a long shot, anyway."

"Oh, honey." Phil walked up to her and pulled her into a hug. "I'm sorry."

Kayla soaked up the warmth of his kindness before pulling away. "It wasn't meant to be. There's something out in this big, wonderful world for me to do, and the universe will fill me in on that someday." She smiled because that belief was so deeply rooted that she couldn't help but beam up at him.

"Always the Pollyanna, aren't you?"

"How can you not be? Every day is a gift, and I'm going to live each one to the max."

"Just like your mom."

"Yep." She nodded. "She may have gone too soon, but she lived two lifetimes in the days she had." Kayla toed up and kissed her uncle on the cheek. "I'll be right back."

CHAPTER 4

Alex leaned back as the doctor worked on his cut. "I could have just superglued it together. That's what we did in the field."

"Hopefully, with medical-grade adhesive," the doctor said as Alex felt his skin tighten. The area was plenty numb, but the tugging sensation was still there.

"If that's what they put in the medical kit, then sure." Alex chuckled.

"What did you do in the military?"

"Ah ... a lot of different things."

"Which is code for you can't tell me." Doc Johnson chuckled. "Okay, then, why did you get out?"

"Injured. Shattered my leg in a training exercise at Fort Benning. I fought for almost a year and a half to stay in, but in the end, I couldn't perform to standards for my MOS. So, they handed me a medical discharge and sent me on my way." Alex felt another tug and watched the doctor's arms move. He couldn't see his hands and didn't really want to. Not that blood bothered him; it didn't.

"Does the leg bother you still?" the doctor asked as he worked.

"It has limits that it doesn't enjoy me going past, that's for sure. And I discovered today that someone jerking on my foot doesn't feel too great either."

The doctor stopped and leaned back so Alex could see his face. The light on the doctor's headband shined in his eyes, and he squinted, hissing and blinking rapidly. "Sorry."

The doctor angled the light up. "Who jerked on your foot?"

"Phil's niece. She thought I was Phil and was playing some kind of joke on him. Or me, rather."

The doctor took off the headband with the light. "Interesting way to greet someone."

"Yeah." Alex closed his eyes.

"I'm going to clean this up. How's your

headache?" The doctor walked to a wall of cabinets and opened one.

"I could use a couple of Tylenol." At least twenty jackhammers slammed against his brain, and the little fuckers didn't seem willing to stop anytime soon. Tylenol wouldn't do a damn thing, but he wouldn't ask for painkillers.

"I bet. You've got a pretty solid concussion there." They'd done the concussion protocol before the doctor had started stitching him up. "I'll give you something. Where are you staying?"

"Number Four." Alex had learned that just giving his cabin number was more than enough for the people of Hollister to know where he lived.

"Ah, Frank is letting you stay there? Cool." Doc Johnson came back with what he needed.

"Frank? I don't know who the boss is, but an acquaintance from my military days hooked me up."

"Somebody from around here?"

"Billy Robinson. He was an instructor at a school I went through."

"I know Billy. He helped me out with a problem once." The doctor fussed over the cut for a moment. "There you go. I want you to take it easy for the next twenty-four hours. If you become nauseous, have problems with your speech or balance, or feel like your light sensitivity is getting worse, come back, and we'll do further diagnostics."

"Got it." The doctor helped him up from the semi-prone position.

"About those headache tablets?"

"Right here." The doctor handed him a cup and moved over to a small refrigerator on the counter, where he retrieved a bottle of water and gave it to Alex. "Take it easy today."

"I've got some small stuff I can work on. Phil has a steady stream of customers."

"By easy, I was thinking of your feet up, your ass on the couch, and listening to your ears ring." The doctor crossed his arms.

"I'd bounce off the walls." Which was true. He wasn't one to sit and do nothing. "I'll be careful."

"Well, at least grab some lunch before you return to work," Doc said. "Gen has Salisbury steak and mashed potatoes today. Homemade bread and veggies. I just finished before Phil grabbed me."

"That sounds good." His stomach gave a grumble of agreement, and he made his way out of the clinic after stopping to thank Stephanie, the doctor's wife, for filling out all the insurance forms for him.

The small SUV in front of the garage was still there when he made his way across the street to Gen's diner. Which meant that Kayla was still at the garage. He stepped into the diner and wasn't greeted by Edna and her little huddle of women. He timed his meals so he'd miss them. He smiled and headed to the bar to sit with Ken, the local deputy.

Ken looked over and did a double-take. "Ouch, dude, what happened?"

"My head met metal, and the metal won," Alex said with a snort.

Ciera whizzed by with his Coke. "You're late. I'll have your plate in a minute."

Alex smiled. He loved the little diner. The food was good and inexpensive, and the staff knew his drink of preference. He took a sip of the soda and sighed. He hoped the Tylenol would kick in soon. The jackhammers hadn't run out of gas, that was certain.

"That SUV over there is packed to the gills and has out-of-state tags." Ken nodded toward the garage. "Are you working on it?"

"Nope. That's Phil's niece." Alex leaned back as

Ciera deposited a platter of beef and potatoes, a helping of green beans, and a plate of warm bread with butter on the side. He cut into the meat and took a bite. The deep beef flavor exploded in his mouth, and the cut was tender enough to eat with a fork. It was damn good.

Ken took a break from his food and looked at him. "Kayla?"

Alex nodded slowly. He didn't want the jackhammers to get mad. "Yeah, dark brown hair, about five-feet-five or so. She's in her mid-twenties." Or at least that was what he assumed. She looked tiny in her big puffy coat, and with her hair pulled up in a high ponytail, he'd wager she was on the lower side of her twenties.

"Yep, I've met her once or twice. I haven't seen her in years, though," Ken huffed and then went back to eating. Alex did the same. When he finished and had another soda, he rolled his shoulders and was glad to say his headache had subsided. "Well, I better get back out on the road." Ken dropped his cash on the counter.

Alex stood and did the same, grabbing his coat from the back of his chair. "I need to get back to work, too."

"Take care. See you tomorrow," Ken said as they left the diner.

Alex didn't nod in case the jackhammers were just refueling. "I hope."

Ken laughed. "Stay away from metal, man. It did a number on you."

Alex burrowed into his coat. "Yeah, she did."

Ken stopped and turned around. "She?"

"What do you call your patrol car? A he?" Alex wasn't going to out Kayla for bashing his skull in.

"Nope, she's a she." Ken headed to the door of his vehicle and waved. Alex lifted a hand and headed next door. He bypassed the gas station and rounded the corners to the maintenance bays. After opening the door, he came to a stop.

"Hi! I'm almost done, and then I'll be out of your way," Kayla said from the desk where he did his portion of the paperwork and looked up parts from their suppliers. She'd taken off her puffy coat, and Alex couldn't help noticing her figure in the t-shirt she wore. He cleared his throat and looked away.

Phil moved to look at him. "How are you feeling?"

"Better. I took lunch before I came back. Stephanie filled out the paperwork for the insurance." He'd hoped to have the bay to himself, but that didn't look like it would be happening any time soon.

Kayla grabbed a pair of scissors and snipped a few threads. "Okay, let's try it." She stood, and so did Phil. Kayla helped him into one arm and flopped the other portion of his coat over his shoulder. She zipped up a zipper on the side and opened the arm of the coat Phil had cut off. That, she fastened around his cast with buttons and loops made out of fabric. At the shoulder, she snapped the opening closed. "There. That should keep you warmer."

Alex moved to get a look at what she'd done and, by doing so, got a perfect view of her backside in those jeans. Man, the woman was tight in all the right places and curved where she should be. He amended his estimate of her age, too. She was probably in her late twenties now that he actually saw her clearly and wasn't looking past a bloody paper towel. "That's a nice job." He blinked and then frowned. Why in the hell had he said that? It had to be the concussion. He didn't give random compliments to people he didn't know.

Kayla beamed up at him. "Thank you! I'll work on those next."

She pointed to his overalls. They were Phil's and about six inches too short and tight. He frowned instead of giving a small shake of his head because he didn't want to rattle his brain about. "No, thank you. These are fine."

She deflated for a minute before that smile popped right back to her face. "Okay. I'll get this mess cleaned up then and go see Aunt Sarah and the girls."

"That's a great idea," Phil said. "I really appreciate this. I was worried I'd catch pneumonia before long."

"I can do that for your shirts, too. I noticed the one you're wearing is held together with safety pins."

Her uncle grimaced. "Your aunt Sarah did her best. She's not exactly best friends with a needle and thread." Phil chuckled.

Kayla's reaction was immediate. "Oh, no. I didn't mean it that way. I'm not criticizing. But I'd be happy to help."

"I know, honey, you wouldn't hurt a fly." Phil glanced at Alex, who was standing like a bump against the wall. "Well, not on purpose anyway."

Kayla's cheeks turned red. "I'm so sorry. It was a practical joke I shouldn't have tried to play."

"I agree. It probably would have given me a heart attack," Phil added.

Alex tried to smile, but he wasn't sure if he managed it. "Your apology is accepted. I'm going to go back and work on that starter and putter around with a few of the smaller projects. I'll get back to that hydraulic system in the morning."

"Why don't you take the rest of the day off?" Phil fell into step with him as he headed to the workbench.

"I'd go stir crazy." As Alex took off his jacket and hung it on a peg by the workbench, Phil turned on a small space heater that would keep the temperature comfortable.

"Then come to dinner tonight." Phil sat down on the old stool.

"It's your niece's first night here. I have a frozen dinner. I'll be fine." He'd gotten adept at dodging last-minute invites. He just didn't feel comfortable altering his schedule, and while he'd probably enjoy the dinner because he'd like to get to know Phil's niece better—without a migraine, that was—last-minute things just made him feel out of control.

Phil puffed out his cheeks. "She didn't mean any harm. You know that, right?"

Alex stopped and turned to look at his partner for the next couple of months. "I do. I accepted her apology."

Phil stared at him for a moment and then nodded. "She's a sweetheart. A free spirit who took care of her mom. Her mom was diagnosed with Parkinson's disease. She and Kayla traveled together after the diagnosis until my sister couldn't manage any longer."

Alex grabbed the starter and a socket wrench. "Sounds like she's had it rough."

"You'd think, but they went places and saw things that most people will never be able to see. Kayla set aside her college and was by her mom's side until she passed about three months ago. She's a damn good person."

Alex stopped and looked at Phil. "I'm sensing you don't think I was serious. I'm holding no grudges. Seriously."

"Then come to dinner." Phil stared back at him.

Alex glanced up to where Kayla was gathering her things. "Listen, Phil, I've worked here for a couple of weeks now. Have you ever noticed me deviating from my schedule?"

Phil frowned. "Huh?"

"I get here at the same time every day. I leave at

the same time. I eat lunch at the same time. I prep for what we have incoming a week in advance. I have a schedule and a way to do things. I don't like it when anyone screws with that flow." Alex rubbed the back of his neck. "And that makes me sound mental, but I'm not. I'm just most effective when I follow a routine."

"How did you make it in the military? That's always changing." Phil leaned his good elbow on the workbench.

"Ha, you'd think, but training was the same. All my missions had the same elements. The command structure was the same. No changes. And when we had a surprise mission, I fell back on the training and the structure in place. I had no problems with life in the military. But if you give me an option, which the military did not, I won't change my schedule without serious consideration."

Kayla went out the door, and it slammed behind her from the wind. "Well, that's making everything come into focus." Phil chuckled. "You could have come out and said that at the beginning. I figured you just didn't like me or the family."

Alex's mouth dropped open. "No, not at all."

"Okay, so if I asked you to dinner next Sunday, would you come?"

Alex set his ratchet down. "Yes, I'd like that." And he would. He enjoyed the family and the food the last time he was there. Plus, Kayla would be there. He paused at that thought but shoved it aside when Phil started talking.

"Good. I'll keep your schedule in mind as we go forward." Phil stood up. "I'll ride home with Kayla and put a note on the front door to call me if anyone needs an appointment. The pumps can be closed for an afternoon."

"If I hear the notification, I can pump gas," Alex said as he opened the housing on the starter. "Do we have any starter springs?" He looked up at Phil. "This one is shot. I'm not sure about the pulley, but I'll be able to tell after I replace the spring."

"We do. Back in the bins, second row from the bottom at the far right. Two or three different sizes." Phil motioned to the back of the garage. Alex nodded and started to the back of the bay. "I'll swing by about closing time and see if there's anything you need to order for these jobs."

Alex lifted a hand in acknowledgment. It took him ten minutes, but he found the spring he was looking for. He worked on smaller projects until closing time. Phil still hadn't made it back, so he left a note on the paperwork that he'd completed and turned off the space heaters and lights. He took off the overalls and put on his coat, leaving off his stocking hat. His head was throbbing now that the numbing agent had worn off.

As he reached for the door, it opened, and Alex stepped back. "What are you doing here?" It probably wasn't the right thing to say, but seeing Kayla at the door was a surprise.

"Uncle Phil asked me to come get the paperwork from your desk. He'll do it at home tonight. He told me to give you a ride home, too. No excuses, and he said he didn't mean to surprise attack you. I have no idea what that means." She bounced on her toes. "It's cold and getting colder. The truck is still running and warm. He told me to plug your truck in, so I did." She moved to the desk. "Is this it?" She looked at the note. "Yep, it is. Come on. Let's go." She opened the door and looked at him.

If his head weren't hurting so bad, maybe he'd have some kind of logical thoughts about the woman in front of him. Her eyes locked on his. The open friendliness and smile on those perfect lips ... Wow, she was fucking beautiful. After the whap on the head, his brain was a bit scrambled. Why hadn't that fact registered better? And why was he thinking about Phil's niece like that? Alex narrowed his eyes and stepped out into the bitter cold. He turned and locked the door using a hasp and paddle lock the size of a platter. He followed her to Phil's truck and got in the passenger seat. Kayla bounded into the driver's seat and put the truck in reverse.

"I have dinner for you, too. I told Aunt Sarah about what I did. We made tacos tonight, so there's a taco kit in that box. Everything you'll need. Just warm up the meat. Uncle Phil included two beers. He wasn't sure if you drank, but he said tonight would be a good night to have a beer." She looked at him as she pulled up to the stop sign. "I have no idea where I'm taking you."

Alex pointed through the intersection. "Cabin number four."

"Which is … this way?" Kayla pointed.

"That way," he confirmed.

"Cool. Anyway, I'm sorry again. You've got a good bruise developing." She made a circle with her finger around her head in the same location as his cut.

"That feels about right."

"Is it terrible?" She bit her lip and grimaced as she waited for an answer.

"Not really. The concussion is something I've dealt with before. I'll be good as new tomorrow. There isn't any reason to worry or be sorry. It was an accident." He was tired, his eyes nearly crossing from his headache, and all he wanted to do was get into the shower for about an hour. Keeping his cut dry, per Doc Johnson's instructions. He wasn't sure how he'd do that, but he would try.

"Oh, I brought you this." She reached into her pocket and pulled out a small plastic bag. He took it from her and pulled out a pink shower cap, which he held up as he looked at her. "Why?"

"Because we ran into Dr. Johnson. He was on the way over to the diner for a cup of coffee with his wife, and he said to make sure you keep the cut dry. It's right at your hairline, so if you wear this, you'll keep it dry." She motioned with her thumb to the back seat. "I also have some dry shampoo in the box and a hairbrush."

What in the hell? Did she really think he'd use the cap or the dry shampoo? Did he look like one of those runway models? He closed his eyes. He was hallucinating. Alex opened them again. Nope, the pink shower cap was still there. What part of the universe did that woman come from? Yeah, she was beautiful but a bit off-center. He shook his head, stopping when his head complained and repeated, "Dry shampoo?"

"Yep. Believe me, it works." She smiled at him and pulled up in front of his cabin. "I'll get the box for you."

"I can—" She was out of the truck before he could finish his sentence. She opened the back and pulled the big covered cardboard box out of the back seat. "Come on." She turned and hit the door with her hip, closing it. Alex sighed. Then he made his way to the cabin door and opened it.

"I can never get over the fact they don't lock doors around here." She walked in, took stock of the small cabin, and walked into the kitchen. "I'll put these containers in the fridge."

Alex took off his coat and hung it on the peg by the door. Kayla was still talking as she worked. "We didn't know if you like soft or crunchy shell tacos. We put both in. The girls helped by shredding the lettuce and dicing the tomatoes and putting everything in the containers. Aunt Sarah made a peach cobbler. She put some peaches up last season when Gen—she's the owner of the diner. I've met her once or maybe twice. Anyway, she got a good buy on ten bushels. Sarah says the cobbler isn't as good as it would be with fresh fruit, but I like it just the same." Kayla pulled out a hairbrush and a spray bottle. "Just point this at your roots and then brush it out. Works like a charm."

His hair wasn't that long, and he hadn't brushed it since before he went into the military. He'd wash it but just tip his cut away from the water. The stitches could take a bit of moisture, and if they dissolved, he'd slap a butterfly bandage on and call it done.

He shook his head slowly, still cautious not to move too quickly because of his concussion. "Thank you, but I don't think—"

"Oh, I know. Men. You'll do it your way, but consider trying the stuff I brought. It'll work." Kayla picked up the cardboard box. "I'll stop by tomorrow sometime and pick up the bowls. Don't worry about washing anything. I'll take care of it tomorrow." She marched to the front door. "Uncle Phil says if you aren't feeling well in the morning, call him, and he'd close up shop for the day."

"I'll be there." He watched as she turned the knob on the door, laughing.

"I told him you'd say that. Enjoy your dinner."

The door closed behind her. "Thank you," he said to the back of the door. He walked to the window and pulled the curtain back a bit. She jumped into the truck, threw it into reverse, and then pulled out toward Phil and Sarah's house.

He dropped the curtain and looked back at the kitchen. "Wow." The word seemed to hang in the room like Kayla had sucked the air and energy out of the cabin when she left. That woman was a dynamo with what so far appeared to be a never-ending battery supply. He wasn't sure anyone could talk that much or that long without taking a breath. But he was pretty sure she managed the feat. He sat down on the couch and leaned back so his neck and head were supported. She was pretty, that was for sure, but dang, the person who decided to take that woman on needed to read the warning label. *Caution. Talks non-stop, doesn't listen, and thinks she knows what's best for you. Beautiful, happy, a smile that could stop traffic, and damn, that tight body.* Yep, it was verified. The crack to his skull had rattled his brain, and he was fixated on that woman. *With reason.*

Alex chuckled and pulled out his phone, dialing Nail's number.

"What's up, Bull?"

"Need any help down there this weekend?"

"Nope, I'm holding on by my fingernails. The following weekend, maybe."

"I have dinner at Phil's on Sunday night next week. If I leave early enough to get back in time, I'm game."

"Damn, son. Look at you all social and shit. Did you have Thanksgiving with them?" Nail laughed, and Alex smiled.

"No. I spent the day reading a book. He invited me the night before, but …"

"I get it. Man, I wish I would have thought to come up."

"You have your family, and they need your focus. I've spent plenty of Thanksgivings and Christmases alone. I'm okay."

Nail was silent for a moment, then changed the topic. "So, why are you going to Phil's next Sunday?"

"He's apologizing for the concussion."

"Say what, now?" Nail got serious quickly.

Alex told him about the crazy woman who came in and yanked his leg. The pain that shot through his reconstructed limb and the concussion. Then he went on to include her stopping by with a pink shower cap and dry shampoo.

Nail's laughter mixed with his. "Shit, dude, is she hot?"

"Hot? Yeah, I guess." She was definitely hot, but he wasn't letting Nail in on that tidbit.

"You guess. Do me a favor and check your pulse, man."

Alex snorted. "I'm alive, and she's attractive. It's not happening, though."

"Why? Hot makes her off limits? Since when?" Nail shot back with the questions.

"I'm not sticking around." Alex shrugged and opened his eyes.

"What's wrong with a little female companionship?" Nail egged him on.

"Nothing. Nothing at all." He hadn't dated since he'd fractured his leg. So, it had been a hot minute since he'd been with a woman. But he wouldn't start a relationship in the middle of nowhere. He could wait until he found a permanent job. Then he wanted it all. A wife, family, kids, and friends. Things his dad had always said were important and that he'd come to value, too. He'd seen happy families in the military. It was hard work at times, but those families were like rocks during a storm. He blinked. Wow, that hit to his dome was making him think shit … He looked for a way to change the subject. "How's Tank?"

"Man, I'm going to kill him before he's released from his doctor's restrictions. Found him in the shop today working on an old Harley that came in. I'm putting locks on the shop door and not giving him a key."

Alex laughed. "No, you aren't."

"Well, I want to. If he pushes it too hard, it'll only take longer to get better. Why the hell can't he understand that?"

Alex's head pounded, and he snorted. "Some of us don't want to admit we're injured."

"Your bean still aching?" Nail was serious again.

"I'm going to take a couple more Tylenol, take an hour-long shower, and then have some tacos and a beer." Alex sighed. That sounded like a fantastic way to end a shitty day.

"A beer, huh? That's unusual. Your bell really must have been rung hard."

Alex chuckled. "The liberty bell has nothing on the crack on my bell. Ten stitches."

"Fuck, dude. Did you lose consciousness?"

"I saw stars and galaxies and a couple of explosions, but no, I stayed awake. Ah, hell." Alex sighed. He just remembered he'd let out a lingo of cuss words when he hit his head. Damn, he needed to apologize. He didn't cuss in front of ladies. Period. That was one thing his dad had instilled in him. No cussing, never strike a woman, and never, ever yell at a woman. Wait until you can control yourself, and then have a discussion.

"Bull, did you hear me? What did you mean by 'ah, hell'?" Alex tuned back into the phone conversation.

"Oh, I just realized I let out a string of cuss words. I'll need to apologize the next time I see her."

"Ah. Gotcha."

They talked for about ten more minutes before hanging up. Then Alex stood up and headed into the bedroom, where he stripped before going into the bathroom. After taking two Tylenol, he stepped into the shower stall, making sure to keep his wound out of the water, for the most part. He relaxed under the hot fall of water. His leg let him know it had been a long day, but that was normal after work. The doctors said his muscles would strengthen and the discomfort would lessen, which it had, but still, that dull ache was there most days. He washed up, using a soaped-up washcloth to rub off all the grease. He loved working on machinery, and the job at Phil's was a dream come true. Phil had himself a little gold mine, and from what Alex saw, he treated his customers fair, and they knew it. No jacked-up margins or added costs came out of thin air. His father had treated his customers the same way.

He missed his dad. His mom had left them when he was a toddler. His dad had said she was too young to be a mom and wife. Alex didn't understand that for a long time, but as he aged and really looked at the world around him, he figured it out. His dad was his hero, his teacher, and his best friend. When his dad died from a massive heart attack, it gutted him. Nail kept him sane. His old man operated in the red, and Alex had to sell the garage to pay debtors, part suppliers, and the bills that had stacked up. It seemed the poor economy had hit his dad hard, but he'd never told Alex.

Alex got out of the shower, wrapped a towel around his waist, and opened the bathroom door. "Oh, shit."

CHAPTER 5

"Oh, shit."

"I knocked!" Kayla squeaked as Alex walked out of the bathroom.

Holy moly and guacamole! His dark skin was ... everywhere. Wow. Her eyes dropped from his face to his shoulders, chest, towel. Oh, man, the scars on his leg. She lifted her eyes again to the *wet* towel that clung to ... *Oh, dear heavens*! Her eyes shot up to his face. His shocked expression had to be the same as the one on hers.

She held up items in her hand. Salsa and sour cream. "Aunt Sarah told me to bring these over. I was going to put them in the fridge. I thought maybe you were asleep?" Kayla wasn't sure if he could understand a word of what she'd said because she'd rattled it off so fast it sounded like one word. It didn't matter. Nope, she was getting the heck out of his house. She turned, set the condiments on the counter, and headed straight for the door. "I should go." She opened the door, slammed it shut behind her, and sprinted to her uncle's truck. Once in the cab, she threw the vehicle into reverse and was out of the driveway.

"Oh my God. Kayla Marie Bryce, you are an *idiot*." She shouldn't have gone into the house. Hopefully, he wouldn't say anything, and they could forget the whole thing. She'd be happy to pretend it didn't happen. That she didn't see ... wow. He was big. His muscles were big, his body was enormous, and the bulge under that small towel was *big*. She slapped her forehead. "Stupid. Oh my God, I can't believe I did that."

Her body tingled from adrenaline and embarrassment coursing through her veins. "Oh, Mom, I totally screwed that up. I know I can't die from embarrassment, but I feel like I could right now. Yeah, yeah, I know I shouldn't have gone in when he didn't answer the knock. You taught me better. I'm such an idiot." Kayla shook her head. She talked to her mom even though she was no longer alive. It was a habit she'd gotten into when her mom could no longer respond to her. She visited and talked without her mom needing to add anything to the conversation.

And she'd really wanted to apologize for hurting him. He seemed ... lonely. Maybe it wasn't lonely. It didn't matter. Any chance of getting to know him now would be useless. She blinked and groaned. "What if he tells Uncle Phil?" She put on the turn signal indicator even though she was the only one on the road. *He wouldn't tell anyone, would he?*

She sighed and slowed down. He might. She didn't know him. He could have thought the situation was funny. But it wasn't. It was embarrassing. What in the world had she been thinking? She knew better than to just walk into someone's house.

Kayla pulled into the drive of Uncle Phil and Aunt Sarah's house. She drew a deep breath and turned off the truck before getting out and plugging the truck into the electrical cord that dangled off the fence. It kept the engine from freezing on those bitterly cold nights. She went inside and took off her coat, hat, and gloves and left them in the mudroom, just outside the kitchen. Toeing off her shoes at the kitchen door, she opened it and was immediately wrapped in the house's warmth.

"That was quick," Sarah said from the counter where she was washing dishes.

"I just dropped them off," she said and grabbed a dish towel, drying the dishes her aunt was washing. "Where are the girls?"

"Doing their homework." Her aunt stopped and cocked her head, listening. "No music, so yes, still doing homework. Alex is a nice-looking young man, isn't he?"

Kayla jerked at her aunt's words. "Ah, yes, he is. Nice guy. Quiet, though."

"Phil says he's not. Says they talk all day about motors and things." Her aunt laughed. "I think he's just shy."

"Shy?" Oh, man. That made her unexpected appearance at his cabin even worse.

"Well, around strangers, maybe. Phil told me tonight Alex hates surprises and doesn't like anything to mess up his routine." Sarah chuckled. "My dad was like that. You could set your watch by the time he walked through our door every night."

"Huh." Kayla had nothing else to say. Alex didn't like surprises. He was shy around strangers and didn't like it when something interrupted his routine. "Oh, Aunt Sarah, he'll never forgive me." She shook her head and put a bowl away. She'd done all three multiple times today.

"For what?" Sarah started scrubbing a pan.

"Everything. I mean, I disrupted his schedule and caused that cut on his forehead. Lord, he has a concussion because of me. If he doesn't like surprises, well, I guess just about everything I've done qualifies in that column."

Sarah chuckled. "I'm sure it isn't as bad as you think. The injury was an accident. Everything else you've done has been neighborly. I'm sure he sees that."

Kayla nodded and took the rinsed pan from her aunt. She wasn't so sure and needed to change the subject. "Oh, if you don't mind, I'll work on some of Uncle Phil's shirts tonight."

Her aunt stopped scrubbing the sink. "I don't want you to come here and work, honey. You're supposed to be resting and recharging."

"Sewing isn't work. I love being able to help, too." She put the pan away and folded the dish towel.

"Sewing isn't work for you. For me, it is." Sarah laughed. "If you really don't mind, I'll go grab the ones we've already destroyed."

"Perfect. Is it okay if I set up my sewing machine on the porch?"

"Yes, and I have a space heater to keep it warmer. We didn't get around to sealing the storm windows this year. Let me go get that heater and my crocheting."

Kayla went to her bedroom and retrieved her sewing machine and the small suitcase containing all her threads, zippers, buttons, and assorted things she'd collected while working as a seamstress. She didn't have a shop but worked from home and had more than enough business from word-of-mouth advertising. The income wasn't a lot, but it paid the utilities and grocery bills. Her mom's insurance covered most of the medical bills, but Kayla had used some of her inheritance to finish paying off what insurance hadn't covered. She had a modest amount in the bank, and now that design school was off the table, she was positive she could live comfortably off the inheritance and any job she could pick up. She wasn't a diva and didn't shy away from hard work. Which reminded her she needed to look for a job after Uncle Phil got out of his cast. She had every intention of helping at the gas station if he needed her.

Not that there were any jobs in Hollister, but she'd keep her ears open.

"Here you go." Sarah carried the shirts, a small space heater, and her crocheting. "I thought I'd sit in here and visit with you while you did your magic."

Kayla laughed. "Crocheting is magic. I've never been able to pick it up." Her little projects ended up looking like shriveled pot holders, which would have been fine if she was actually making pot holders, but she wasn't.

"Well, I guess we each have our talents." Sarah plugged in the heater and placed it between them.

She took the first shirt and looked at the seams. Salvaging the shirts would be easy. It took a moment to find a matching color thread and bobbin. "Where's Uncle Phil?"

"He's asleep in front of the television. He won't admit it, but it's hard for him with his arm in a cast. That foam brace helps, but it makes things awkward. The operation and the worry about the shop really took a toll on him. Thank God for Alex. We were going to pay him fifty percent of the profits, but he wouldn't take it. He said with his medical retirement, twenty-five percent was more than enough."

Kayla looked over her sewing machine at her aunt. "He refused to take money? I mean, who does that in this day and age?"

"Right? We were in shock. It seems he's a godsend," Sarah agreed.

He was a lot more than that. A nice guy. One who was hurt. She lowered her eyes. He'd survived whatever had caused those terrible scars on his leg. She couldn't imagine the pain he'd endured. Yet he gave up money so Phil and his family would be okay. "That's really nice." The understatement of the decade, but what else could she say that wouldn't make her sound like a love-sick schoolgirl?

Sarah's hands flew as she wound the yarn around the hook and weaved it through the rows she'd already completed. "He's a good man, and Phil says he's one of the best mechanics he's seen. Some of the new stuff is foreign to him because he was in the military and didn't get updates, but he searches the internet and finds what he needs to fix them."

"The military?" That would explain Uncle Phil's comment about his leg having a ton of hardware holding it together and the scars.

"Yes. The Army, I think he said." Sarah pulled

another arm's length of yarn and settled back into her work.

"Do you think that's where he hurt his leg?"

Her aunt looked up and frowned. "I didn't know he'd hurt his leg."

Kayla worked on a seam but nodded as she guided the material. "Uncle Phil told me he had a lot of hardware in his leg. I didn't ask then, but being in the military would make sense."

Her aunt made a sound of agreement. "He made an impression on you, didn't he?"

Kayla glanced up, and her face heated. "I don't think he'd ever look my way."

"Why not? You're beautiful, inside and out." Her aunt dropped her hands to her lap.

"I'm not. I'm pretty ordinary." Kayla smiled at her aunt. "But thank you for the compliment. That's sweet."

Sarah lifted an eyebrow but let the conversation drop, and Kayla was thankful. She worked on her uncle's shirts, lost in the work's familiarity. As the thread went through the material, her mind slipped back to the last time she had a boyfriend. Almost eight years ago. She was twenty-eight now. Sure, she'd dated occasionally, especially before her mom's condition advanced, but it had been a long time since she'd had a crush on someone.

Kayla lifted her foot from the pedal and stared at the material she was threading through her machine. That was the second time she'd thought that. A crush? Yep, that was what was going on, wasn't it? Wow. How did that happen? She didn't have a clue, but the fact was she did think he was attractive—and more so after the towel sighting. She closed her eyes and shook her head.

"Something wrong?" Sarah's voice shattered her thoughts.

"What? Oh, no. I was just thinking." She pushed the pedal to start her machine again and tried concentrating on the fabric she fed through the needle and thread. It worked for about two seconds before she was thinking about Alex again. The rage she saw on his face when she bent down to look at him under that thing he was working on stuck in her mind because, when he saw her, his demeanor changed instantly. He didn't raise his voice. He was a bit grumpy, to be sure, but she couldn't blame him. And when she wiped out and landed on her butt in front of him, he was more worried about her than himself. *That* told her a lot about his character.

She cut the thread and trimmed the seam before reaching into her suitcase for some soft hook and loop material to use as a fastener. As she placed the backing of the material on the seam, she concluded that she needed to bite the bullet and apologize.

CHAPTER 6

Alex unlocked the door to the garage and turned on the lights. The walk to the garage had been brisk, but the wind wasn't blowing too badly. He made his way back to the heaters and cranked them up. It usually took about thirty minutes to get the place warm enough to work, so he locked the door behind him and made his way to the diner.

"Hi, Alex. I'll be with you in a minute!" Ciera yelled from the kitchen. "Grab a cup of coffee."

Alex dipped his head at Doc Macy, who was already eating breakfast, and headed to the cart beside the counter. He poured a large mug of coffee and added cream and sugar.

"You're here early." He sat at the counter beside the veterinarian.

"A milk cow got herself into a tussle with a barbed wire fence. Had to do some fancy stitching, but the old girl will be fine." Doc did a double-take at him. "Speaking of fancy stitching, what happened?"

Alex chuckled. "My brain tried to evacuate the premises yesterday. Doc Johnson sewed me together."

"Concussion?" Doc Macy narrowed his eyes and looked at the wound. "You hit something hard."

"Well, that's the truth. I hit it hard, and the metal undercarriage wasn't inclined to move in the slightest. Doc Johnson said I had a concussion. My headache told me that before he did." Alex chuckled.

"You best be careful. Most of that big equipment could squish you." Doc Macy shook his head. "Don't need another person running around in a cast."

"Ain't that the truth?" Alex leaned back as Ciera appeared with his biscuit and milk. "There you go. Anything else today?" She smiled at him, and Alex pointed under his eye.

"You've got some—"

She swiped at her cheek and laughed. "Well, nobody ever said I was a tidy chef. That's a preview of lunch."

"Which is?" Doc Macy asked before taking a bite of his sausage biscuit.

"Individual beef pot pies." Ciera made a big circle with her hands. "Could serve two, but with the appetites around here, they're single servers."

"I'll be here," Alex said before biting into his egg, cheese, and ham biscuit. The cheese melted and gooey, the meat a thick slab cut off a country ham, none of that paper-thin spiral-cut stuff. The biscuit was almost the size of his plate. He'd had it the first morning before he went to work for Phil and never switched it up. The food at the diner was homemade, filled him up, and kept him warm and focused on his work.

The bell rang, and both he and Doc Macy looked back. Ken Zorn nodded at them as he wiped his boots on the rug at the door.

"I'll be right out, Ken," Ciera called.

Ken said nothing as he made his way to the coffee urn and sat down next to Alex after pouring a large mug full of the brew. "Morning." The deputy mumbled his greeting.

Alex finished chewing his food and glanced over at the guy. Bags the size of suitcases hung under his eyes. Alex's eyebrows lifted, but that hurt, and he stopped the movement. He took a drink of his milk and asked, "Long night?"

"Damn straight. Some asshole decided he could drive across the country with bald tires. Ended up in the ditch. Me and the state patrol waited for the tow truck with this guy and his family. I can't imagine taking such a risk with small kids."

Alex shook his head. He'd seen desperate people do desperate things while he was overseas. "Sometimes you got no choice, man. Sometimes you do what you have to do."

Doc Macy nodded. "He knows. He's just venting."

"I gave the guy a hundred dollars so he could get the tire fixed. He's being towed back to Belle because it was closer. SDHP is following with his family while he rides with the tow truck. The tow truck is only charging the guy for gas." Ken dropped his cowboy hat in the chair beside him. "Troy Flores was telling me he put in his retirement papers."

"Really?" Doc Macy leaned forward, and Alex

edged back so the guys could visit. "They're going to replace him, right?"

"Yep. He said one trooper from around Pierre volunteered to move to this side of the state."

Ciera came out and put a bacon biscuit and a cinnamon roll in front of Ken. "The roll is on me. I heard you pulled an all-nighter. Carbs will help you sleep."

"Thank you." Ken smiled up at the woman.

She winked at him and headed back into the kitchen. "I have to get these crocks covered before the crowd comes in. If you need anything, let me know."

"Damn, it's going to be a long day." Ken pushed the cinnamon roll over toward Alex. "Take half of that, please. I have to sit through a meeting in Belle this morning, and I don't need to fall asleep driving down there."

Alex cut half the roll off and then put half of what he took on Doc Macy's plate. The man said nothing and dug in. Alex took a sip of his coffee before asking, "Can't you phone it in or have someone else brief you on what's going on?"

"I could. But this is a briefing from a multi-jurisdictional task force the governor has put together. They're working on several cases, and getting the scoop in person is worth the lack of sleep. Otherwise, the updates get funneled through other people, and shit always gets lost in translation."

Alex took a sip of his coffee and eyed the clock. He still had about ten minutes before the garage would be warm. On the way back, he'd open the front of the business and unlock the pumps. He finished his biscuit before commenting, "A special task force. Sounds ominous. Is there a lot of crime around here?"

Ken shrugged, chewing as he spoke. "Depends. We have our share of dishonest people. Arguments that become physical, husbands and wives who shouldn't be married and act out. Robbery? Not so much. Phil's garage was broken into a while back, but they were trying to run him off his land. No murders that I'm aware of."

Alex snorted. "Good to know about the murders. Nail … ah, Brian told me about Phil's situation. I take it his land is valuable?" He put his fork through the roll and took a bite.

"Yes and no. Ranch land is valuable. All this land belongs to Senior except Phil's land and the acreage the Bit and Spur is on."

Doc Macy interrupted. "This diner, too."

"Hollister land now." Ken snorted. "She's married to Andrew, and Senior is her father-in-law." Ken took another bite of his food.

"Senior would be Andrew Hollister. He and Frank Marshall own most of the land out here." Doc filled Alex in.

Ken nodded and continued, "Right. Hollister owns it all except the Bit, Phil's land, and the acreage between his house and the garage, which is where Gen's garden is."

Alex cocked his head. "Garden?"

Doc Macy answered because Ken took another bite. "Yeah, that big, plowed field behind the garage. That's Gen's vegetable garden. She uses all the produce here and gives away what she can't use, can, or freeze, cutting the cost for all of us. Phil rents her the land for a pick of the produce. His wife Sarah is a damn excellent cook, too, and her root cellar is full of canned veg, fruits, and such."

"I know that. She sent her niece over last night with a taco box. All the fixings and a peach cobbler. It was good." Alex had decided the brief encounter last night was funny, but it took his bruised brain a hot minute to put humor into the situation. He'd bet dollars to doughnuts that Kayla wouldn't open his door without an invitation anymore.

"Because you bumped your head? Damn, I need to do something klutzy." Ken chuckled at the stink eye Alex threw at him.

"Her niece?" Doc Macy said. "Oh, I didn't realize she was here already."

"Arrived yesterday," Ken Zorn, still laughing, informed him.

"How's Phil doing?" Doc Macy asked.

"Good. That cast bothers him. But I think he's finally trusting me to do the work. He didn't leave my side for a solid week." Alex chuckled. "But I can't blame him. He's got a reputation to uphold, and he didn't know me from Adam."

"Few people look at the other person's point of view these days," Doc Macy said as he sat back. "I'm going to head over to the office. I have clinic this morning."

"Do they bring in cows?" Alex asked.

Doc Macy barked out a laugh. "Nah, small animal clinic. Dogs, cats, hamsters, things like that."

"Oh." Alex laughed. "Man, I was trying to work out the logistics of a cow at the clinic."

Doc Macy clasped him on the shoulder. "I'll

never get that image out of my head." He laughed as he dropped his cash on the counter. "See ya."

Ken got up and poured himself another cup of coffee. When he turned around, his shoulders dropped. "Head's up. Here comes Edna and the girls."

Alex lifted his milk glass to his mouth, tipped it up, and finished it in one draw before standing up and dropping his money on the counter. "Thanks, man." Edna and her hen party had caught him once before—Ken's description of the ladies, not his. It was painful, and it took far too long for him to excuse himself politely from the inquisition.

He put his jacket back on and opened the doors for the ladies. "Good morning." He smiled at each of them, and before Edna could ask what happened to his head, he was out the door and heading to the garage. She'd probably catch him sooner or later, but he wouldn't make it easy for her.

He opened the pumps, turned on the lights and heater in the front of the business, then made his way back to the big bay, where he opened up and checked for any phone messages while turning on the computer and confirming the status of the parts Phil had ordered. When he was done, he pulled on a pair of Phil's overalls and headed back to the job he was doing when he cracked his head open yesterday. Alex pulled the tools he'd need and set them on a big plastic tray that he could slide without scratching the tools. He found the mechanic's creeper and laid down. The plastic under him was damn cold, and a chill went down his spine, but the plastic would warm up; the cement floor wouldn't. He grabbed the undercarriage and pulled himself under the vehicle. *Where was I?* He glanced up and then reached over to his plastic tray.

Alex was just finishing the truck when he heard the door open. Phil was a bit late that morning, but that was his prerogative. Alex perched himself precariously on his knees at the edge of a semi's engine compartment and focused on pulling the glow plug wires so he could remove the plugs and clean and ream them before replacing them. He pulled off the wire he was working on and spoke at the same time. "Phil, you can write up the Swenson's truck. No change in the time or parts from the estimate."

"Ah, I'm not Phil."

Alex lifted and glanced over his shoulder. Kayla stood quietly a distance away. He moved and sat down on the truck, elevated high above her. "No, you're most definitely not Phil." She was five feet and a couple of inches of woman. All woman, even under that puffy white coat. He remembered that all too well.

She looked down and moved the toe of her shoe on the concrete. "I came to apologize. Again. I told Uncle Phil I'd offer you a ride to work, but you'd already left."

Alex chuckled, and her head jerked up. He held up a hand. "It's okay. It was a shock to see you standing there."

"Yeah, a shock. That ... that's how I'd describe it, too." She rolled her eyes and then looked at the ceiling, speaking to it instead of him. "I'm not a pervert or something. I was just going to leave those containers in your fridge."

Alex laughed at that comment. "I didn't think you were being pervy. You would have had to stick around longer to be classified that way."

Kayla groaned. "Please, can we keep this between us?"

All the levity left as he looked at her. "I would never embarrass you by saying a word about what happened last night."

She glanced at him. "Thank you."

He made his way off the semi, being careful not to land on his bad leg. "What are you doing here so early?"

She shrugged. "Besides giving you a ride and apologizing, I wanted to stop at the store when it opens to see if Allison has any elastic. I'll go down to Rapid sometime soon and shop for the stuff I don't have."

"What are you working on? More shirts for Phil?" He grabbed a rag and wiped off his hands.

"No, I finished them yesterday, but Christmas is coming up, so I was going to make the girls some new clothes and a quilt for Phil and Sarah. The one I made them years ago doesn't match the new color they painted in their room, but they're still using it." She snapped her mouth shut. "But you didn't want to actually know that."

Alex frowned. "I asked, didn't I?"

Kayla shrugged again. "I'll go now. I just wanted to make sure you knew I was sorry for barging in on you last night." She turned to walk away.

"Hey, what's up? You're different today."

She dropped her head to her chest before turning around. "You don't like surprises. You don't like your schedule messed with, and you're shy. You must hate me for what happened yesterday."

Alex chuckled and rubbed his neck. She had him pegged, didn't she? Seemed the sexy little package in front of him was doing some homework. Who had she been talking to? Phil. Without a doubt. But she had a few facts completely wrong. "Well, the introduction could've gone better."

She laughed. "That's for sure. How are you feeling today?"

"Better. My headache is gone." Alex closed the space between them. Her hair was down and fell to her shoulders in thick brown and gold waves. His fingers itched to run through her hair, but he'd never risk getting her greasy. Not that he had the right to touch her. "How are you feeling? You fell pretty hard yesterday."

She rolled her eyes. "Fine. I have plenty of padding." She lifted her coat as evidence. "I'm sorry for interrupting your day, seriously."

"Stop apologizing. Look, I'm working on being more flexible with my schedule, but that's not going to happen overnight, and I'm not shy. I never have been, but I'm not exactly a chatty person either. And I guarantee I don't hate you."

She looked up into his eyes as if to see if he was

telling the truth. He lifted four fingers. "Scout's honor."

She laughed and lifted her hand, showing him the correct hand signal. "That is scout's honor."

"Oh." He fixed his fingers. "Better?"

She smiled brightly. "Much. I'm going to go have a cup of coffee and wait for Allison to open up. Have a good day, Alex."

"You, too. Don't be a stranger." He watched her walk away, unable to stop from noticing the swing of her hips. She stopped at the door. "I won't be, but I guarantee I'll wait for an answer before I walk into your cabin again."

"That's probably a good idea." He waved and headed back to the glow plug wires. He smiled and hoisted himself up into the engine compartment. Somehow, he felt lighter, happier than he did before she'd visited, and no, he wouldn't look too closely at the whys of that feeling. He'd just enjoy it while it lasted.

CHAPTER 7

Kayla opened the door to the diner and wiped her feet on the rug as she looked around. "Kayla?"

Edna Michaelson stood up from the booth. "I thought you were supposed to be here today. Come sit down with us."

Kayla took off her coat on the way and sat down with the women. "I was waiting for the store to open. I need elastic." She smiled at the waitress, who came over with coffee. "Thank you."

"Kayla is Phil's niece. This is Ciera. She lives above the diner with her husband and son. Kayla's been here with her mom several times. Oh, I'm so sorry about your momma." Edna put her hand over Kayla's.

"It's okay. She was suffering, and we had a long goodbye." Kayla smiled. "It's nice to meet you, Ciera."

"It's nice to meet you, too." Ciera winked at her and smiled. "Can I get you some breakfast?"

"No, coffee is fine. Thank you." She'd eaten already, and she remembered the size of the servings at the café.

"Let me know if you change your mind or need rescuing from these ladies."

Edna and the ladies laughed, not insulted by the comment. Kayla figured it was some kind of inside joke.

"What do you need elastic for? I have several bundles at home," Belinda Pratt said quietly from the back of the booth.

"Oh, I thought I'd start on the girls' Christmas presents."

"You sew?" It seemed all the ladies said the words at the same time.

"Yes, I'm a seamstress."

"I can bring the bundles by Sarah's today if you'd like."

"That's so kind of you. Let me pay you for them."

The woman smiled sweetly. "I'm not using it,

and it would have ended up in the trash sooner or later."

"Thank you." Kayla would make the woman an apron. She had plenty of scrap material that she could use.

"Wait. Can you quilt?" Doris Altham said from across from her.

"Oh, definitely. I was thinking about making a new quilt for Aunt Sarah and Uncle Phil for Christmas. *Please* don't let that cat out of the bag." Kayla looked around the table.

"Never," Edna assured her. "We have a crocheting and knitting circle, but we've been reading books about quilting. The patterns seem so hard."

"Oh, it can be intimidating, but I can help you learn."

Edna beamed. "We can meet at the community hall. That way, Sarah won't know you're making one for them for Christmas. She doesn't sew, but she does crochet with us at the church."

Kayla allowed herself to be swept away with the enthusiasm. "That would be nice, but I'd have to work all day every day for a week or so to finish the quilt in time for Christmas. Would that be okay with the people who own the place?"

"Absolutely. We can be there to help, too. We can arrange our schedules, right, ladies?"

"Perfect. Oh, I'm so happy. I was wondering how I could make the girls' clothes and the quilt for Aunt Sarah and Uncle Phil. This works out very well, actually."

Edna snapped her fingers. "Wait, why don't we ask Melody if Kayla can use one of the side rooms until after Christmas? They have nothing scheduled, do they?"

"Hold on." Doris pulled out her phone. "According to the social media page, we have the Christmas decoration and tree lighting. There's a town Christmas party, depending on weather, of course, and a New Year's Day celebration and potluck."

Edna tapped her fingers on the table for a second. "Don't forget the dance."

"Right. A fancy dress dance. Suits and ties for the gentlemen and dresses for the ladies." Belinda smiled widely.

"Using one of the side rooms shouldn't be an issue. I wouldn't think. I'll call Melody."

Kayla jumped into the conversation that was going faster than she was comfortable with it going. "Wait, I really don't want to pay to rent a space."

"Pay? No, sweetie. You won't have to pay. You can set up in there, and you can teach us quilting. I'm sure as soon as word goes out that you're willing to help us, a lot of people will want to learn."

"If you're sure." Kayla felt like she was being pulled along by a force she wasn't sure she could resist.

Edna made a pfft sound and dialed her phone. "Hi, Mel. How are you and the boys?" Edna smiled and then laughed. "How about me and the girls come out this afternoon and let you come into town and visit with adults?" She looked across the table, and Belinda and Doris nodded in unison.

"Perfect. Hey, the reason I called was Kayla Bryce, Phil's niece, has come to stay with Phil and Sarah. Anyway, to make a long story short, she's volunteered to teach us how to quilt." Edna was silent for a moment. "I know. I'm so excited. But listen, she needs a place to set up where people can work and there's space. What? Yes, I thought about one of the side rooms. If she needs more room when people find out she's teaching, she can open the partition. Ah, okay. About the service charge."

Edna smiled and winked at Kayla. "She'd be glad to teach you how to quilt. Heck, we should all bring our sewing machines in and set up so we can work there. Yes, I know. The kids could play in the rowdy room while we learned how to put those patterns together." Edna nodded. "Okay, I'll let you break it to Declan. See you this afternoon about two? All right, sweetie. See you then."

Edna put down the phone and beamed. "There, everything's settled. I'll let you know when we can set up, and we can discuss the dates you want to start. I'm so glad you stopped in and we stayed a bit later than usual."

"Well, there was a reason." Belinda pointed at the camera on the table.

Edna rolled her eyes. "Darn it, it won. I can't get my film to rewind in this camera. We've tried everything except opening the back. I don't want to lose the pictures I took, but goodness, they've been on the camera forever and a day. The place I send them off to might not be able to develop them."

Kayla took a sip of her coffee. "Film, it's not a digital?"

Edna shook her head and pursed her lips, and

the other ladies mimicked her movement. "Oh, no. I'm a purist."

Kayla blinked in surprise but was able to stifle the laugh the comment spurred. Which was good because she'd hate to hurt the woman's feelings. "Ah, may I?" She motioned toward the little black camera.

"By all means. It has us snookered." Edna moved closer. "You flip this little lever out, and you're supposed to wind the film back into the canister. But it just spins."

Kayla flipped the little silver toggle out and tried to rewind it. "It isn't doing anything."

Doris sighed. "That's what we've been running up against."

"You know, I bet Alex would know how to fix this." Kayla smiled. "Either him or Uncle Phil. Both of them are great with all kinds of mechanical things. May I take it next door? I can give it back to you when we meet up at the ... Where was it again?"

"The community hall. It's behind the Bit and Spur, but you don't need to go through the bar to get to the hall. There's an entrance on the other side." Edna preened a bit. "I'm not averse to having a drink. I'm not a prude, but having a place to have wedding receptions, town events, and such was an excellent idea. Declan Howard may have been a rake at one time, but Melody has turned him into a steadfast family man. He built that hall for the town." The women around the table nodded in solidarity.

Kayla took a sip of her coffee and raised her eyebrows in surprise at the amount of information that erupted from Edna.

She swallowed. "Oh, okay. So, I can see if they can make this work?"

"Absolutely." Edna glanced at her watch. "Ladies, we need to get to the crocheting circle over at the church." Kayla slid out of the booth, and the ladies followed suit, slipping on coats, scarves, hats, and gloves. "See you tomorrow, Ciera!" Edna yelled to the back of the kitchen.

The woman came to the door. "Enjoy your day, ladies."

"Oh, we will. We always do." Edna led the procession out the door as Ciera watched, shaking her head and smiling. "They can be overwhelming."

"They're nice. I've met them several times. My mom used to enjoy visiting with them." Kayla sat back down in the booth.

"Would you like me to warm that up?" Ciera asked with a nod toward her mug.

"Please." Kayla accepted gratefully, then had a thought. "Wait. Are you ready to close? I can leave."

Ciera came back with a cup and a thermal pot. "No, we don't close in case someone needs a frozen dinner or something. We stop breakfast service in about an hour. Lunch starts at eleven-thirty, and it'll be busy today. Beef pot pies." Ciera sat down and poured herself a cup. "So, are you moving to Hollister?"

"Temporarily. I need to find a job, eventually. My mom passed, and I have some money saved, but I don't want to be a burden to Uncle Phil and Aunt Sarah."

Ciera stirred some sugar into her coffee. "What do you do?"

"I'm a seamstress, and somehow, I've been recruited into teaching Edna and the ladies how to quilt." Kayla laughed. "That was unexpected."

"Really? I'd love to learn how to sew on a machine. I have clothes I could fix. I can darn, and I'm good with a needle and thread, but some of these things need a machine because the fabric is too thick for a needle and thread, no matter how strong the thimble is."

Kayla blinked and drew back. "I can do that for you. I'll show you how to use a machine, too, but I can fix those clothes in a heartbeat."

"Really?" Ciera sat up straight and glanced at the clock. "I can run up and grab the little box that I put them in. I'll pay you."

"No, you don't need to do that. It really isn't that hard," Kayla said as Ciera rose from the booth.

"Nope, I'm paying you. If you ordered something from the diner, you'd pay for it, right?"

"Well, yeah."

"See, that's what I'm talking about. Fair is fair. I'll be right back. If anyone comes in, tell them to have a cup of coffee, and I'll be right down."

The woman was out of the front of the diner before Kayla could say anything. She picked up her coffee cup and whispered to herself, "Well, girl, you've made some serious plans this morning, haven't you?" She looked out the window. Her uncle was pumping gas. At least he was warm in his coat while he was doing it. He was such a relic. Heck, coming up to that small town, she seemed to step back in time. People there didn't lock houses or vehicles. They left strangers alone in diners with the cash register and gave them cameras without a second thought. It was ... really nice. She took another sip of coffee.

Ciera came back a few minutes later with a box of clothes. "This looks like a lot. Maybe it is, but I couldn't throw them away. I'm a penny-pincher. My husband is trying to get me to ease up on it, but I went through a rough spell, and I can't seem to get over hoarding perfectly good clothes. Well, not perfect, but they could be again." She laughed.

"Well, let's see what we have." Kayla pulled out several shirts, jeans, a coat, and a sweater. She looked at the sweater closely. "Would your son be averse to me putting a series of patches, making it look like it was supposed to be there? It's about the only thing I can do with these thick double knits."

"That would be fine. He doesn't care. I tried to darn it, but he keeps tearing it out. The yarn is slippery, almost like a nylon, and the darning stitch can't grip."

"I can see that. What's he interested in? I can cut the patches in shapes. Planes, Trains ..."

"Can you do horses? Scott took him to the ranch, and he's head over heels with the horses out there."

Kayla nodded. She could download a royalty-free image and make the patch look like a horse.

Oh ... "I can add a mane and tail with some embroidery thread. White would show up great."

"Really? You're so talented. I'll pay you for this, by the way. No arguments."

"We'll see," Kayla said under her breath. She enjoyed helping people, and she didn't need the money right now.

CHAPTER 8

Alex rubbed his hands together as he headed toward the front desk. It was bitterly cold that day, heck, the entire week. There weren't many people out and about, and he couldn't blame a soul for staying tucked in where it was warm. The door opened and slammed close behind Phil. "Damn, can it get any colder?" the man muttered as he entered.

"Don't ask that. The powers that be might take it as a challenge." Alex sniggered and plopped down beside the heater.

"We'll have a fully functional heater before long. The one I ordered is due in next month. Damn near seven months to get here. With all these supply chain issues and other excuses, getting anything made overseas has been a nightmare. Thank God things are normalizing." Phil sat down in the chair beside Alex. "We're going to lock it up today. These space heaters aren't cutting it."

Alex chuckled. "I'll be fine. I have to finish the Hollister's job, and then a Mr. Kinzer called and wanted to know if you or I could come out and look at his milking machine? I got to say, that's one I've never heard of before."

"Ah, damn. If that milker's down, those cows have to be milked by hand. I won't be able to fix a damn thing, but I'll take you out there. We should leave now. We didn't promise Senior his rig back until next week. Morning milking is done, and they'll have cleaned up already. You game?"

"If it's a machine, I'll take a stab at it." Alex wouldn't put a milking machine on his resume, but it would be a challenge.

The door opened again. "Hey." Kayla bounced into the bay. "Uncle Phil, do you know how to rewind one of these things?" Kayla extended her hand to him.

"Damn, it's been a hot minute since I've seen one of those. Where did you get it?"

"Edna gave it to me last week, and I forgot I had

it until today. I feel terrible about forgetting to ask if you could fix it."

Phil looked at it and nodded. "There's a silver tab. Pull the little handle out."

"Like this?" Kayla moved the little toggle switch out.

"Yep, now, pop it up one notch."

"Pop what up?"

"The silver winder," Phil said.

Kayla looked at the winder and then at her uncle. "Ah ..."

"Here." Alex took the camera and lifted the silver circle. An audible click sounded.

"There you go. Now, wind it counterclockwise," Phil said.

Alex tried to hand it back to Kayla, but she held up her hands and stepped back. "You've got the touch."

Alex chuckled and wound the little spindle until it wouldn't move any longer. "Pull it up again," Phil said. Alex lifted the little silver toggle again, and the back of the camera popped open. "There you go."

"How in the world did you get Edna's camera?"

Alex handed Kayla the little canister from inside the camera and then the camera itself. She put them in her pocket as she answered her uncle. Alex chuckled at how Kayla described the tidal wave of Edna taking control and her having a quilting class to teach. He could see it happening after his experience with the woman. Plus, Kayla was kind, so she'd never duck out. He listened to her talking about the conversation at the diner. Her face was animated and glowing. Her eyes flashed, and that smile, if it ever turned on him, would knock him on his ass. Alex rolled his shoulders. Damn, he didn't need to be thinking about Kayla like that, especially in front of her uncle, aka, his boss. A bit of a tangled web ... or not. He was leaving as soon as Phil could turn a wrench again.

"Are you okay with that?" Phil asked her. "I saw you working on a box of clothes last night."

"Yes, I want to make some things for Christmas, and this way, I can do it without the girls and Aunt Sarah seeing what I'm doing." Kayla clapped her hands. "I'm going to have to make a run down south to get some material and a few things. I'm so excited." She practically radiated in front of them.

"Well, girl, you don't let those old ladies take advantage of you. You hear me?" Phil stood up. "We have to go out to the Kinzers'. The milking machine is down, and if Charlie and Doug can't fix it, it's complicated."

"House calls? That's nice," Kayla said. "I can stay here and pump gas. I have nothing else to do right now."

Alex frowned, and Phil shook his head. "Nah, it's too cold. I told Alex we're going to call it today, but the Kinzers need help."

"Okay." She looked up at the clock. "It's still early. Aunt Sarah is at her crochet circle, and the girls are at school. I'll take this back to Edna, pop down to Belle Fourche, maybe go over to Spearfish to check out what type of fabrics and such they have."

"Do you have your cell phone? Is your vehicle full of gas? Do you have a cold winter kit?" Phil rattled off the questions, and Alex crossed his arms. He didn't know why, but the thought of her traveling that distance in the cold bothered him.

"Yes, yes, and yes. I'm no fool, Uncle Phil. I'll be back by suppertime." She toed up and kissed him on the cheek. She waved at Alex and was out the door.

Phil looked at him. "Why do I feel like I should've let her pump gas?"

Alex sighed. "Not sure, but I'm not too keen on

her traveling on her own." That protective vibe was a leftover from his time overseas and unwarranted in the States. Yeah, he needed to chill out. He put his hands on his hips. "And that is misogynistic, isn't it?"

"Well, son, I'm not sure what that means, but if it means overprotective and just a bit caveman, then yep, it is."

Alex snorted and grabbed his coat. "Close enough."

* * *

ALEX SLID out from underneath the engine that ran the milking machine. He and Doug Kinzer had basically rebuilt the thing. Luckily, the Kinzers had some spare parts. What they didn't have, Alex could bypass or rig it so the electric engine would work until the additional parts came in. Hopefully. He'd seen engines die, but that thing had imploded. Of course, he found out it ran every day, twice a day, and was rarely serviced. "Okay, start it up." He nodded to Charlie Kinzer, Doug's dad. The man straightened his shoulders and flipped the switch that started the system. The system powered up. Alex glanced back at the motor. "Hang in there, baby. You can do it."

"Are you talking to the motor?" Elaine Kinzer asked.

"You bet I am. If it goes out again, I'm not sure we'll be able to patch it up." Alex got up. The milking barn was warm and unbelievably clean. He was expecting ... Well, he wasn't sure what he was expecting, but not the setup before him.

"Thank you, young man." Charlie Kinzer offered him a hand.

"You're welcome, but I've got to tell you that this system is on its last leg." Alex hated to be the bearer of bad news.

Charlie nodded. "Know it." The man put his hands on his hips. "But I ain't paying for a new one till this one goes out."

"Mr. Kinzer, that could be any minute." Alex laughed. "I can put in the parts we ordered when they come in, but that engine is Frankensteined together. It won't last."

Phil snorted. "Open that vault you store your wallet in, Charlie. Get a new system here before this one quits. We'll install it for you. Or rather, Alex will install it for you," Phil amended.

Dana Kinzer, Charlie's wife, walked up behind

him. "We'll order it tonight. I'll let you know when it's coming in. We can run the milk lines and such, but we'll need help to switch out the main system."

"You'll need an electrician, too." Alex wiped off his hands. "I can work on motors, electric, gas, or diesel, but the wiring from the power source to the engine needs to be done by someone with more smarts than I have."

"We can call Tegan. He's good with wiring," Elaine said, and Alex could have sworn she blushed. Then again, it was warm in the barn.

Charlie nodded. "What's the bill for this?"

"Alex?" Phil looked at him.

"Well, since Doug helped and everything…" He glanced back at Phil. He really didn't want to charge the Kinzers. "It's not going to last."

Phil nodded. "No charge this time, but we'll charge our hourly labor for the install."

"That's mighty kind of you. Hold on a second, and let me get you a couple of gallons of milk and some cream. Elaine, come help me."

"Thank you." Phil smiled as the women hurried past. By the time Alex had stowed his tools and cleaned up, they were back.

"Tell Sarah I'll stop by with some eggs tomorrow. The hens are warm in the henhouse Doug built them, and they're laying like crazy."

"That's mighty kind of you." Phil took Alex's tool bag, and Alex wrapped his arms around two glass gallon jars and two quarts of cream.

Alex perched the milk between him and Phil and the cream he put on the floorboard by Phil. Alex hit the windshield wipers to wipe the two inches of snow that had settled on the truck while they were working. The defroster struggled for a bit to clear the window, but they could drive away after about five minutes. The snow was coming down hard, and it was blowing. "Damn. Phil, I don't like the fact that Kayla is out in this weather," Alex said as they pulled onto the highway. There were a few drifts forming across the blacktop.

Phil leaned over so he could see the clock. "She should be on her way back now." He pulled his cell phone out of his pocket and dialed. "Hey, where are you?" Phil looked over at him. "You're doing what?" Phil growled. "I'll come to get you."

"What's going on?"

"She's changing a tire."

"Tell her to stay in the truck and keep warm. I can go get her with the tow truck."

"Good idea. Alex is coming for you with the

tow truck. We can change the tire in the garage where it's warm. Get inside your vehicle." Phil was silent for a moment before speaking in a tone that Alex hadn't heard before. His *Dad* voice. "Kayla Marie Bryce, I'm not arguing with you on this. You'll freeze before you get those damn lug nuts off. Do you hear me?" Phil grunted. "Good. Alex will be there. Make sure your exhaust stays clear," Phil grunted and then hung up. "Her teeth were chattering like crazy."

"Where is she?" Alex pushed the gas as fast as he could, considering the road conditions.

"About forty minutes south of here." Phil shook his head. "Why in the hell didn't she just call?"

"She's independent?" Alex guessed. "She doesn't want to be a burden? She's crazy?"

Phil laughed. "Probably yes to all three. That young lady … She wanted to go to school to learn design for clothes and such. Her momma took ill, and she put that on hold. When she applied after her momma passed, she couldn't get in. She'd give a stranger her last dollar and be happy as a lark because she could help someone, never mind that it left her with nothing." Phil shook his head. "She's her momma's daughter, that's for sure."

"Sounds like your sister was a good person."

"She was. Practically raised me because of our age difference. Kayla is a good person. I know you two got off on a bad foot."

"I told you we're good." Alex slowed down and made the turn into Hollister.

Phil said, "I'll double-check everything is locked up and head home. Call me if there are any problems. I'll be worrying, but I'll just be in the way with this damn thing." He lifted his casted arm.

"I got this." He'd be driving a class C tow truck, which was basically a semi. Phil's truck was old but in pristine condition. Alex parked and pointed at the milk. "Don't break those. I've never had fresh cow's milk."

"Then you're in for a treat. Go get Kayla, and after you put the truck in the front bay, come for dinner." Phil held up his hand. "It's the least I can do because you're not getting any pay for this afternoon."

Alex shrugged his shoulders. "We'll see."

Phil nodded. "All right. I'll take that."

Alex opened the front of the gas station, grabbed the keys to the tow truck, and then locked the business. Phil's truck was just taillights by the time Alex had finished brushing the snow off the massive tow vehicle. Then, he jumped into the semi, turned the key, and waited for the glow plugs to warm. He used the ice scraper to clear the windshield of a layer of ice before getting back into the truck. The light for the glow plugs had changed to green. He cranked the engine and shoved the machine into gear. His bad leg bitched at him, but he didn't give a fuck. He moved through the gears and told his leg to shut up. Damn it, he knew she shouldn't have driven that far.

The massive vehicle trundled down the highway, and Alex tried to shove down the anger he was feeling. Not at Kayla, but at himself. He had no right to tell Kayla what to do. None. *Then why in the hell was he so pissed?*

CHAPTER 9

Kayla sniffed and wiped at her runny nose. The bitter cold was vicious. She pulled the blanket from her emergency kit around her tighter. When she stopped because her tire was making clunking noises, she'd turned off her SUV and set her emergency brake. When Phil chastised her, she'd gotten back in, but it wouldn't crank. Not a growl, a groan, or a whimper. Not even a click.

She'd never had a problem with her SUV before. It was a reliable and well-maintained vehicle. Yet there she was, watching her breath puff out of her mouth. The windshield was obscured by snow. She had her emergency flashers on, but they, too, had stopped. Kayla ate one of the chocolate bars, which was almost frozen. She let the chocolate melt on her tongue and hoped the sugar would help to keep her warm.

She heard a big truck's horn and poked her head out of the blanket to see Alex had parked across the highway. She watched him climb down from her uncle's tow truck. He limped quickly across the highway and was at her door before she could open it.

"Why in the hell isn't your car running?"

Kayla jerked back. Alex was angry. She pointed to the engine. "It wouldn't start."

His lips clamped together tightly. "Come on, get in the truck while I turn it around and hook you up."

She kept the blanket around her, still holding her semi-frozen chocolate bar, and staggered as he all but pulled her out of the little crossover SUV. The wind cut through her long coat and the blanket. It got cold in Utah, but not that cold. She fumbled at the steps into the truck. Alex's hand planted on her ass and pushed her up. She landed halfway between the two seats with an unceremonious grunt. He was up and in the cab by the time she could scramble into her seat. As she futzed with her blanket and chocolate bar, he made a three-point turn and then backed up in front of her vehicle.

"Stay here." Alex cranked the heat to maximum and left, slamming the truck door behind him.

"Like I was going to go back outside?" She would've made a face at him, but she was too cold. Kayla huddled closer to the vent, pulling the blanket over her enclosing the heat under the blanket. She was shaking like a leaf. The cold was no joke. When she heard the winch whine, she moved away from the vent and back into her seat.

The clanks and clinks continued as Alex attached her vehicle. About five minutes later, he opened the truck door. After climbing in, he sat huddled in the seat, saying nothing. "Do you want my blanket?" She was warming up, still cold, but she had to be warmer than him.

"No." He took off his gloves and reached his hands out to the heater vents on either side of him. "It looks like the rim sliced the wall of the tire."

"I always check my tires, just like Uncle Phil taught me. They're only about a year old."

"I saw. It's probably a manufacturer defect. The wall wasn't as thick, and when you drove in the cold, the air contracted, giving the rim an opportunity to work on that spot. Why did you have to go today?"

Kayla blinked at him. "Why not? Did *you* know it was going to be this bad?"

Alex turned to look at her. "It *is* South Dakota."

She blinked. "Well, that's true. I would've been fine if I hadn't turned off the vehicle."

"Why did you?"

"I turned it off, set the emergency brake, and got out my spare and lug. I don't need my vehicle on to change the tire. I'm not an idiot." She was getting a little defensive.

Alex sighed and put on his seat belt. "I'm sorry. When I pulled up and didn't see any exhaust, I thought maybe the snow had choked it. You could have been dead from carbon monoxide poisoning." He placed both hands on the massive steering wheel, closed his eyes, and drew a breath.

Kayla glanced back at her little SUV. "You were scared, not mad."

"Mad?" He turned and looked at her with a puzzled expression.

She'd never had anyone scared for her. Well, maybe her mom and dad, but those roles changed when her mom was diagnosed. She took over as caretaker and chief worry-wart. It was unexpected to be worried about now, but really, really nice. She took a deep breath and soaked that feeling in. She nodded. "When you yelled at me."

"Did I?"

She snorted. "You absolutely did."

"Well, I'm sorry about that. I wasn't raised that way. Put your seat belt on. We should go."

She pulled the strap across her chest and lap and buckled it.

"Did you find what you were looking for down south?" he asked as he signaled the truck to go back on the highway and sped up. She saw him wince when he shifted.

"Does it hurt? Driving a stick shift?"

"Doesn't feel good," he admitted.

They were silent as he drove. She'd finally stopped shivering and could relax back into the seat. Closing her eyes, she rode, listening to the rumble of the big truck and the sound of the heater pushing hot air into the cabin.

"You didn't answer my question."

She popped her eyes open and oriented herself. "I'm sorry. What did you ask?"

"Did you find what you were looking for?"

Oh! "Yes, some of it, but I'll have to go to Rapid.

I could match Aunt Sarah and Uncle Phil's room color. Three different shades of blue, with the room shade in the middle of the quilt shooting out in a star pattern. I can't wait to start work on it. I need to hustle to get it done by Christmas. I also found some denim for jeans and jean jackets for the girls." She'd also found material that she would line with flannel to make Uncle Phil and Alex new overalls. The ones they had were ready for the garbage bin.

"I'm going to Rapid Friday night after work to help my buddy out in his shop. I'll drive us down. He wanted me to work both Saturday and some of Sunday, but I can come back on Saturday."

"Oh, well, I can get a room for two nights." She had enough money in her budget to rent a room for a couple of nights. Plus, she'd love to take her time and look through all the stores to see if she could find bargains. Usually, the fabric stores sold irregular and last-of-bolt cuts on the cheap. She could check to see what they had and bring some back for her quilting class.

He glanced over at her. His brow furrowed a bit. "You wouldn't mind?"

"No, not at all, and if we took my SUV, I could drive around to all the stores while you worked. I could pick you up when you're ready, and we could drive back." She almost vibrated in her seat. Actually, it was perfect. She could do all her Christmas shopping next weekend. She wouldn't spend a lot and would make most of her presents. Despite that, going for the weekend was a fantastic idea. That way, she wouldn't have to go back down south until after Christmas. She'd have to find work, but she was giving herself until January before she started looking.

"If we get it running, that sounds like a plan. Was it the battery?" Alex asked as he drove.

"I don't know. There was just nothing there. I mean nothing. Like there wasn't a battery. The ignition didn't even click, and the emergency lights weren't going."

"That's ... strange," Alex said, but he wasn't looking at her. She turned to look at what he was. "Oh, that's a nice motorcycle." The old pickup in front of them was hauling a motorcycle in the truck bed. A blue tarp flapped in the wind, showing the motorcycle as they drove down the road.

"It's strange that it's not covered. That's a custom ride." They slowed as the truck approached the Hollister exit, and the other truck continued north. They bounced through town, and Alex backed into the automotive garage's drive. Kayla got out to use his keys to unlock the garage and roll up the door. Alex unloaded the truck, and they pushed it back into the garage. Kayla shut the roll-down door and got her purchases out of the truck. She stood looking at the bags when Alex came in to hang up the tow truck keys. "I've started my truck. I'll run you back to Phil's. What did the bags do to you to piss you off?"

"Huh?"

"You look mad," Alex explained.

"Oh, no, I'm not, but I don't want to spoil the surprise."

"I'm not following." Alex leaned against the wall, his weight on his good leg.

"If I go in with these bags, the girls will want to see, and so will Sarah. It's a girl thing. We're curious."

"And?" Alex prompted.

"And if they see, they'll know I'm working on something for them." She sighed and looked back toward her SUV. "I should just leave it here and come back for it."

Alex stood away from the wall and picked up

the bags. "You can keep it at my cabin. I have an extra room I'm not using."

"Really? Thank you. That would make things simpler." She followed him and locked the business up before giving him back the keys.

"We'll stop there before we go to Phil's. They invited me for dinner, and I want to return the containers you delivered."

She turned to him. "I never came back for them, did I?"

He chuckled. "No, and I can't say I blame you."

They got into the old truck, her bags between them. "I'm sorry." She wasn't sure what she was apologizing for that time, but it seemed like she should do it again.

Alex put the truck into gear and laughed. "Don't be. You test my self-imposed plan to be more spontaneous."

"Yeah, how's that going for you?" Kayla laughed at him.

"I'd say I'm failing, but I won't let that stop me from trying." Alex pulled into the drive for the little cabins. "Come in. I'll show you where you can set up."

"Set up?" She jumped out of the truck he'd left

running and stepped through the snow to reach the door.

"You can use this room." He opened the cabin door and stomped off his boots on the rug. She followed suit and then trotted after him. "It's warm and private, and your aunt, uncle, and cousins don't come here. Plus, I'm not here Monday through Friday, so you'd have the place to yourself."

"Oh!" She blinked and looked at the tidy little room. It had a desk she could put her machine on. She could use the community hall, but this option was preferable. Plus, there was the delay in the quilting class start date because of the weather. Driving from the ranches in the bitter cold was frowned on, and now, she knew why it was discouraged. Lesson learned.

But ... she had two machines, her new one and her old workhorse. She could set up the new one there and use the older one when they worked on quilting. "Are you sure you don't mind?"

"I wouldn't have offered it if I did. Think of it as me exercising my spontaneity." Alex pointed down the hall. "I'm going to go change my shirt."

Kayla laughed. "I can wait in the truck."

"Nah, I'll be right back." Alex winked at her, and

then he was gone from the doorway. Kayla smiled and hugged herself. She left the room and shut the door behind her, moving into the little living room. She sat on the couch and looked at the stack of books beside a small table that held the lamp. "Oh." She picked up the top one and read the back cover. A thriller. Wow, she'd like to read it.

"It's good. I picked up a bunch of them at a thrift store in Rapid but didn't have time to read them while I was working at the motorcycle shop." Alex spoke as he walked out of the bedroom.

"Wow." The word slipped out of her. "I mean, I like that sweater." The fabric hugged his chest and arms and made him look like an Adonis on steroids. Good God, the man was so attractive. She'd seen him almost naked and knew how big he was, but the soft material of the sweater implied what was underneath, and that was so, so sexy.

"Thanks." He brushed his hand down his flat stomach, trailing over the soft brown fabric. "I've had it for years. One of the few things I have that is nice and still fits."

"Oh, it fits." She put the book down. "Ready?"

A smile spread slowly across Alex's face. "Are you?"

"Yes." *For anything, everything.* Goodness, her

thoughts were all kinds of inappropriate, but it was so easy imagining slipping into his arms.

"So am I." He winked at her again and grabbed his coat. "Let's go."

Kayla shivered as his hand touched the back of her coat. *That* shiver wasn't from the cold.

CHAPTER 10

Alex pulled his boots on and frowned at the sound of a vehicle outside. He walked over to the window and pulled back the curtain. Phil's old truck pulled up out front. Kayla popped out and walked to the passenger side of the truck.

Alex opened the front door as she marched toward the cabin with a large plastic case in one hand and a small suitcase in the other. "Do you need help?"

"Good morning! No, I'm fine. I thought I'd take you up on your offer, but Uncle Phil said you go to work at an ungodly hour, so I wanted to make sure you were home when I came by. Just so you knew I'd be here today." She marched past him, stopping only to stomp off the snow from her shoes.

Alex shut the door and shoved his hands into the pockets of his jeans. Last night's dinner at Phil's was fun. He'd admit that. Kayla was a riot and had everyone laughing about her misspent youth and the things she did to be cool. The picture she'd pulled up on her phone of her hairstyle in the late 2000s was beyond ridiculous, and yet the woman owned it. He smiled as she walked back into the living room. Kayla stopped short. "What?" she asked.

"I was thinking of that hairstyle."

"Hey, I looked good with kinked and crimped hair. It was the bright pink and blue eyeshadow that made it work." She made a face at him, and he laughed again.

"I'm going to get breakfast. Care to join me?"

Kayla squinted her eyes and cocked her head. "Are you being spontaneous this early in the morning?"

Alex laughed. "No, I'm following my routine. You'd be the one being spontaneous."

"Oh, then, absolutely. I'll take my uncle's truck because I'm not walking farther than I have to in this cold."

"Sounds like a plan. I need to open up the garage and get things warming up. Then I'll be over at the diner."

"Perfect. See you soon." Kayla bounced out of the cabin. Alex couldn't prevent his smile at her energy. He turned off the lights and followed her outside. He had to warm up his truck and scrape the windshield, so he was several minutes behind Kayla. Parking in his usual spot, he went about his morning routine. When he made his way into the diner, it surprised him to see Ken and Tegan in the booth with Kayla.

"Hi!" She waved and scooted over so he could sit down.

"Good morning." He nodded to Ken and Tegan before grabbing a cup of coffee from the cart. "Kayla, would you like some more coffee?" he asked from across the room.

"Oh, yes, please." She bounded out of the booth with her cup. When she sidled up to him, she got close and leaned over to push the lever to dispense the coffee. The scent of her hair or perfume or soap or whatever the fuck it was hit him full force. He drew a deeper breath. There was so much about this woman that called to him. She was mesmerizing.

"They kind of invited themselves," she whispered as she grabbed three sugar packets and two creams.

Ah, well, he got it. Hollister was a small town. They were being *friendly*. He mentally rolled his eyes. The guys were being guys. He slid in after Kayla and stared at the other two. "Kayla, I see you've met Tegan. He runs the stockyards. This is Deputy Sheriff Ken Zorn. The law in these parts."

"We met several times over the years, and I'm not actually the only law. We have a state trooper who cruises through now and then." Ken chuckled. "I'm sorry to hear about your momma, by the way."

"Oh, it's okay. She lived a wonderful life, and she was ready at the end." She smiled and took a sip of her coffee.

Tegan smiled at her. "How long are you planning on staying in Hollister?"

"Oh, probably through January. I need to find a job. I have a small inheritance, but I want to use that wisely and not burn through it, you know?" She chuckled. "I don't think Hollister needs a seamstress."

"You're a seamstress?" Ken blinked and then blurted, "I have uniforms that need to be altered. I get new ones from the county, and they're huge to fit the bullet-proof vest. Talk about a balloon. I have to take them to Rapid to get them tapered. Do you think you could alter them?"

Kayla blinked. "Sure."

Tegan nodded. "The work you'd have might surprise you. I know some of the women who ride barrels go down south to commission shirts. Then there are the ladies who enter the rodeo queen events. They want matching suits. You might want to consider opening a little shop."

"Really?" Kayla looked up at Alex. "I may be at your cabin more than I expected."

Alex leaned back as Ciera came out with four plates and Alex's milk. "You're staying with Alex?" Ciera asked.

"No, when I'm at work, she's using the spare room in my cabin to work on her Christmas gifts for her family, so they don't know what she's making." Alex wanted to stop any rumors right off the bat.

"Oh, that makes sense. The ladies of the town are talking about the quilting class. I know several are really serious about it. Kathy Prentiss—she teaches school—wants to attend. She makes curtains and a couple of seat cushions, but she said that was just straight seams and squares. She wants to learn how to read a pattern and make things."

"I'd be happy to teach her anything she wants to learn."

Ciera glanced around. "More coffee, anyone?"

Alex shook his head. Kayla pointed at her biscuit. "Dear heavens. Could you bring me a to-go box now? I could eat this for lunch and dinner."

Ciera laughed. "Will do." She left and headed to the bar to take an order from the guy who managed the hardware store. Alex tried to peg the guy's name. Schmidt. Carson Schmidt. The guy turned around and lifted his coffee cup. Everyone except Kayla acknowledged him. She focused on cutting a quarter of her biscuit from the rest of the meal.

"See, you should think about sticking around." Tegan shrugged. "We don't have a clothing store up here. Nowhere to grab a pair of jeans without making the trip down south."

Kayla stared at him for a moment. "I think you just gave me an idea." She looked up at Alex. "Do you know if there's any storefront space available?" Her eyes traveled to Ken and then to Tegan.

"No, everything is pretty much used up here. Doesn't mean you can't find someplace, but I'm not aware of anything," Ken said before taking a bite of his food.

"Oh." Alex watched her shoulders fall, and he nudged her leg with his. She looked up at him. "We can talk about your idea and put our heads together. Maybe we can come up with something."

"Really?" Kayla brightened up again. "Okay, let me flesh out the idea, and we can talk about it when we go to Rapid for the weekend."

"Sounds like a deal." He took a bite and looked up. Ken's eyebrows rose. Alex rolled his eyes and shook his head no. The guy smiled and took another bite of his biscuit. Alex ate and listened to Kayla visit with the guys. The feeling in his gut was akin to irritation. It irritated him that Tegan and Ken sat with Kayla. He was also irritated because that fact irritated him. He took a drink of his milk. Kayla laughed, and he watched both Ken and Tegan. She hypnotized the guys. He could see why. Kayla sucked everyone around her into the energy she created. She was regaling Tegan and Ken on how she was the cause of Alex's stitches. If there was anything else in the universe, neither Ken nor Tegan could see it. Kayla reached over and placed her hand on his leg. An innocent gesture, to be sure, but damn if that didn't puff his chest up.

Kayla asked each of them what their most embarrassing public display of gracelessness was. He laughed when Tegan talked about falling head over heels from a horse in the middle of a grand parade. The road rash hurt for a couple of days, but his pride had never recovered.

Ken Zorn declined to comment. "I'll pass for the moment. What about you, Alex?"

"Ah, that would be banging my head against the undercarriage and needing ten stitches."

Kayla rolled her eyes but laughed as much as everyone else.

Alex finished his milk and glanced at the clock. He had a few more minutes to visit before he needed to go to work. He threw his arm over the back of the bench. A very animated Kayla described in detail how she ran back from the workbench and slipped because of her wet shoes and did a double gainer, planting on her bottom.

"Welcome to Hollister, Kayla." Tegan laughed as he spoke.

"Right? Within two minutes of pulling into town, I've caused bodily injury to my uncle's godsend and bruised my backside. I tell you, it *has* to be some kind of record."

"Well, gents. It's time for me to go to work."

Alex got up and dropped enough money for Kayla's breakfast. "My treat."

Kayla scooted out of the bench seat and looked at the money. "Okay, well, tomorrow morning is my treat."

Ciera appeared and handed Kayla a white box. "Here's your to-go container."

"Thank you." She slid the biscuit into the cardboard box and looped her hand through his arm. "Time to go to work."

Alex couldn't help the smile. The possessiveness of that gesture was probably a show for the other guys, but he didn't care. He'd enjoy the little act while it was happening. He grabbed his coat at the door and slung it on while Kayla put on her hat and gloves. When they walked out, she asked, "Do you go to the cabin for lunch?"

"No, I normally eat here." Alex stopped them before they walked past the building as it was a windbreak, and the cold wasn't as intense.

"Okay, well, I guess I'll see you tomorrow morning. My treat, remember."

Alex cocked his head. "Tomorrow sounds good, but I'm not letting you buy my breakfast." Yeah, that was his ego talking, but the way he was raised stood up and pounded on its chest.

Kayla moved closer to him and squinted her eyes at him as she looked up. "That's really old-fashioned."

"The Army would call it misogynistic, but it was how I was brought up. The men pay for meals."

"If you're on a date, right?" She still stared up at him.

"Right."

"This was a date?" Her left eyebrow arched. Just one. *How in the hell did she do that?*

Alex looked down the street, steeling himself for what he would say. He wouldn't be around for long, but he wanted to know her better. He needed to know her better, and although he didn't understand the urge, he would run with it. "Did I invite you?"

She nodded her head. "You did."

Alex shrugged. "Then it was a date unless you don't see it that way."

She stared at him and pursed her lips. Finally, she admitted, "I *can* see it that way."

"Unless ..." He looked down at her and then back toward the diner. "Do you want to go to breakfast with someone else?" He shoved his hands in his coat pockets.

Kayla's eyes popped open, and she glanced toward the diner's door. She looked up at him and then smiled. "No, I don't want to eat with anyone else."

"Then, it seems like it was a date." He wasn't shy, not by anyone's standards, but that was quick work, even for him.

"Huh." She crossed her arms over her chest and looked down the street again. "Well, all right." She nodded and stepped off the boardwalk, heading toward Phil's truck. She stopped and came back, stepping up on the boardwalk. "Tomorrow is a date, too?"

Alex smiled and nodded. "It is."

"I usually kiss my dates goodnight if I've had a nice time." She toed up and kissed him on the cheek. "Thank you."

She spun again and headed straight toward the truck. Alex watched her go. A smile split his face, and he wouldn't hide it. She waved as she backed out of the parking spot, and the truck headed toward his cabin. Alex blinked, pulling himself out of whatever trance he was in, and headed to work.

He was dating Kayla.

Alex walked over to Phil's garage and finished opening up before he went to work in the bays. He was dating an extraordinary woman. She was vibrant, filled with excitement, and the dynamo she was, made him happy. He closed the door behind him and grabbed a portable heater. Blessing's words floated through his mind. *"Give spontaneity a chance when you get to South Dakota. I promise you; it will lead to good things."*

Well, damn. Maybe it would.

CHAPTER 11

Kayla sat in the running truck, staring at the little cabin in front of her. "Well, that was unexpected. I'm dating. In Hollister. Who would have ever thought that would happen?" Her words splintered the silence of the cold surrounding her in her uncle's truck.

The man she was dating was sexy and great company when he didn't have a concussion. A shiver went up her spine and traveled down her arms. She felt the sensation in her core. "Hollister. Of all places." She turned off the truck and got out. After plugging in the truck so it wouldn't freeze, she mounted the steps and wiped off her shoes on the inside doormat. Then she leaned back against the door and closed her eyes.

It was toasty warm in the cabin. Kayla took off her hat, gloves, and jacket and hung the coat on a peg by the door. She slid out of her shoes and padded into the guest bedroom. The little room was warm and snug. After taking the lid off her sewing machine, she placed it on the desk and plugged it in. The light illuminated the makeshift workstation. Kayla looked around. She'd need a flat surface to cut patterns out. The counter separating the kitchen from the living room would work. She could cut out her patterns right after Alex went to work. Then she could clean up the area, and he'd never know she'd used it.

But first, she had an idea to write down. She pulled out her phone and called up a blank note. Sitting on the bed in her new sewing room, she typed out the ideas she'd received from talking with Tegan and Ken that morning. A small place where she'd have a proper sewing environment with a table she could use for patterns. She had serging machines and embroidery machines in temporary storage. She stopped and stared unseeingly at the wall in front of her. If she took in clothes to alter and repair, perhaps she could make a few things to sell *and* run a consignment shop. Kids always outgrew clothes; people bought clothes that didn't fit or that they didn't like. A consignment shop would put a little money into the pockets of the town, too.

What else? Kayla dropped back on the bed and stared at the white ceiling and the decorative light. How could a seamstress make a living in a place like Hollister? Quilts. She could make those and sell them. Winter was a bear up here, and heavy quilts could be a good seller. Her mind hopped from one thing to another, and she dismissed several ridiculous ideas. But she could advertise tailoring for rodeo clothes, and … she sat up. Things like weddings, although she'd need a lot of notice for bridal gowns. The last gown she'd made had taken forever. The beading, in particular. But she could sit beside her mom and talk to her while she did the work, so she hadn't minded the tedious task.

Was there enough population to support something like that? Maybe if she stocked some jeans in popular sizes. Well, it was an idea. But there were so many variables. Having a location and the space to set up shop was the primary concern.

She sat up and looked at her watch. She was meeting Edna at the community center at ten.

Until then, she'd get to work on the outfits she wanted to make for the girls.

* * *

"And this is the room where you can set up and sew," Edna said as she led Kayla through the community hall.

"I'll just need the area for quilting lessons. I have a place to sew now." Kayla looked for electrical outlets. There seemed to be plenty.

"What? Where?" Wide-eyed, Edna spun and stared at her.

Kayla blinked. "Oh, that's right, you don't know. Alex goes to work every day, Monday-Friday. He offered me the spare room in his cabin to work on the Christmas presents I want to make. It's perfect, and I won't be inconveniencing the entire town by using the center, and on the off chance that if Uncle Phil or Aunt Sarah stop by, they won't see what I'm doing."

"Oh, well, I guess that makes sense." Edna huffed a bit. "You're still doing the quilting classes, though, right?"

"Absolutely." She would keep that promise.

Edna nodded. "We talked about it in the crochet and knitting circle and at the weekly ladies of the church meeting. We think everyone should pony up five dollars for each lesson." She held up her hand when Kayla tried to object.

"Five dollars a lesson is ridiculously cheap, we know, but it's something that everyone around here can afford."

"No, I wasn't going to object to the price. I wanted to tell you that I don't want to charge."

Edna pulled out a chair and sat down, nodding to another chair. "This is why I'm here alone. We didn't want you to feel we ganged up on you, but …" Edna sighed and crossed her arms. "Around here, you have some mighty prideful people. Mighty prideful. Most would love to do something like learning to quilt, but if they thought it was a handout, they'd stay at home."

Stunned, Kayla's mouth dropped open. "You're joking."

"No, ma'am, I'm not. Now, you can set it up however you want, but I'm telling you, just putting a jar at the door would be the way to go. I'll be paying. Every woman I know will do the same."

"But … I was trying to be neighborly." She didn't want people to pay to learn how to sew.

"And you are, believe me. Some ladies know a lot, some don't even know how to thread a sewing machine, but everyone has one. You'll earn that money." Edna laughed and then waved. Kayla turned around. A woman with a baby on each hip walked in. "I'm sorry I'm a bit late, but Scott had a blowout that required a bath." The woman laughed and jiggled one baby. He smiled. A very tall and very broad blond man came in behind her. He took one baby and smooched him loudly.

"Baby break." He put his arm over the woman's shoulder. "You must be Kayla."

Kayla stood up. "I am. Thank you so much for letting us use the room for quilting lessons."

"I'm Declan Howard. This is my wife, Melody. That is Scott, and this is Jared."

"Nice to meet you." Kayla smiled at the twins. "How old are they?"

"Almost one," Melody answered. "We love having something to offer to the community. Your class fits the vision we had for the space."

Declan nodded. "That's why we built it. We've sponsored a Fourth of July picnic, a Harvest potluck, and a Halloween party for the kids in the area. We're always looking for other ways to support the town."

"She'll need it one night a week. She's got another place to do her Christmas gifts and such." Edna walked over and took the baby from Melody. "How about a kiss for Aunty Edna?" She smooched the child's cheek, then blew a raspberry on his neck, which caused a shriek of laughter.

"That's fine. We're going to get some of the teenage girls to come and babysit for those of us who need it. What night were you thinking of doing the class?" Mel asked as Edna gave Scott to Declan and took Jared to give him love and kisses.

"I don't have any idea. What would work best for everyone? Wednesdays?"

"No. Amanda and the girls from the Marshall ranch can't do Wednesdays. They have a standing appointment with the Winchesters that night." Edna rocked back and forth with the baby in her arms.

Kayla blinked. "I really don't know what that means."

Melody laughed. "Neither did I, but don't worry, you'll learn. What about Thursday?"

Edna nodded. "I think that would work. Don't you?" She asked the baby and got a huge smile and babble in return. The boy then let out a string of *daddadadada's* and reached for Declan.

"That's my cue, and I need to get back to the other side of the business. I'll take them and watch them." He took the baby from Edna and headed toward the back of the building.

"Call if you need me," Mel said as Declan retreated.

"Take your time. I got this," he replied, disappearing into a hallway.

"He's a great dad." Edna sighed. "I always knew he would be."

Mel looked like she was trying not to smile and winked at Kayla. "You called it. He's the best. Now, what do we need to do for the class?"

"I was looking at power outlets. Everyone needs to bring a machine if they don't know how to use it. I am going down to Rapid this coming weekend to get some salvage material and odds and ends. We can practice on that. Of course, I'm hoping to find a variety of cake layers and charm packs."

"I have no idea what that means. Are we cooking or sewing?" Melody laughed.

Kayla laughed. "Oh, sewing for sure. I'm not much of a cook, but hanging around Aunt Sarah, I hope that changes. Cake layers are actually packages of fabric that are already cut into ten-inch squares. Charm packs are five inches square. It makes life easier. If you're sewing on point, you can cut the squares with a rotary cutter and ruler while using a sandpaper circle to make sure it doesn't slip. I have a rotary mat, so we won't need to get one of those. I'm also going to pick up as many patterns as I can. They're inexpensive, and if we're careful, we can use them more than once. The internet has some excellent resources, and people can download a pattern they like for a couple of dollars and print it up. Most of the pieces are small enough to print on a sheet of paper. The edging, batting, backing, and such we can do with measurements and making sure we sew and set the seams properly."

"Okay, so the first class needs to be a definition of terms and learning everything you just said."

"Which would work out because I need to go to Rapid to buy the materials, and I'm not charging for that first class." Kayla lifted a finger at Edna. "No arguments. It's a 'come see what you're getting yourself involved with' class."

Edna laughed. "All right, all right. I concede that point."

"Good." Kayla hugged herself. "I'm so excited about this."

"I'm glad. Between the two churches and the circles, I think about fifteen to twenty women are interested. I'll put the word out that this Thursday is a 'come and see' meeting."

"I can't wait." Mel clapped her hands. "I know Steph, Allison, Gen, Ciera, Corrie, and Kathy are all interested."

"Besides the rest of the town regulars, Amanda and Keelee said that there are several out at the ranch who would love to learn, so we should have a good size class." Edna glanced at her watch. "I do need to run. The girls and I are heading down to Belle Fourche to do a little shopping and drop off that film you were able to get out of my camera. And thank you for that."

"The guys did it. I just watched so I could show you. I'm sorry it took so long. I just forgot I had it."

"Girl, that film has been in that camera forever. There's no need to be sorry. As soon as you showed me how to rewind and open the darn thing, it all came back to me. It's been years since I used that camera, but I took it out and played with it. Don't ask me why. The girls and I went just out of town and shot the wildflowers, the antelope, and I even got close enough to a bee on a flower to get a wonderful picture. I don't like bees," she said as a way of explanation as she headed to the door, wrapping up in her coat, hat, and gloves as she went.

"Well, I'm sure they're wonderful," Kayla said to Edna's back as Kayla put her coat back on. "Thank you so much again, Melody. Are you sure you don't want me to pay?"

"No, if it's for the community, then it's free. If you were having a big function with food, drinks, and such, then we'd rent it out. Events like that where people want to decorate and make sure they're the only ones with access so they can leave things and have them secure." Mel shrugged. "It works for us and the town."

"Well, thank you. Hey, Edna, we didn't discuss a time for Thursday night," Kayla called after her.

"Seven," she called back. "The girls and I will spread the word." She waved as she walked out the door.

"That woman is a force of nature." Kayla laughed.

"She is, and she's wonderful with a heart as big as the sky. She's accused of being a busybody, and to an extent she is, but I think mostly she's lonely, and doing everything she does makes her less so."

Kayla nodded, staring at the door. "Loneliness is painful."

"It is," Melody agreed. "Speaking of which, the next time the girls get together, we'll invite you. Usually, it's at Gen's diner after they close. It's a central location. We generally bring a bottle of wine and visit or play card games. Canasta. We're using three decks of cards. Shuffling is a production."

"I've played Canasta. My mom taught me before she became too shaky and couldn't hold the cards anymore." Kayla laughed. "She was a card shark."

"Well, then, you'll fit right in. Give me your cell phone number, and I'll call you when we all converge."

Kayla exchanged cell numbers with Melody and headed out. She was pretty sure Edna had overestimated the ladies who would be interested in learning to quilt, but she would teach them whatever they wanted to learn.

She cranked her uncle's truck up and waited for the defroster to kick in before she drove past the gas station and onto the cabin. She smiled and looked up at the clear blue sky. Finally, it wasn't gray and dark. "Momma, I like your hometown." She smiled and blew a kiss heavenward before heading into the cabin to start working on her Christmas projects.

CHAPTER 12

Alex visually assessed his toolbox and made sure all of his tools were in place before double-checking the work order for the tractor he'd been servicing. Word had gotten out that Alex would do routine servicing on all tractors, and those who hated fighting to replace belts or didn't want to deal with the old oil after changing it out were bringing their equipment to Phil's.

There was a steady stream of work. Alex had jobs lined up for the next month, and by the sounds of the phone, he'd have a few more scheduled. He wiped his hands and made his way to where Phil was pecking at the computer with his left index finger.

"Need help?" Alex asked as he dropped into the chair beside his employer slash partner.

"Nope. I may be slow, but I'm doing something useful and contributing. I feel like a total slacker."

"You shouldn't. I get what you're saying, though. I hated it when I was in the hospital and then my cast. I felt like the world was moving at warp speed, and the plaster hobbled me." Alex chuckled and leaned back in his seat. "The tractor is done. I replaced three belts we didn't quote. I kept them so they could see the wear and dry rot. They'd have shredded as soon as that thing started any heavy work."

"Good, I always keep them to show the customers, too. Never want to be accused of padding a bill."

They sat in silence for a moment before Alex asked, "So, if a person wanted to take a girl out around here, what's available?" Alex had been thinking all day about what to do besides breakfast and lunch. Hollister was not big by any stretch of the imagination, and he didn't know what kinds of things were available.

Phil sat back and looked at him. "Would I know this person and the person he wants to take on a date?"

"You would." Alex nodded, giving him only that.

"Would it be my niece?"

"It would."

"Well ..." He leaned back in his chair. "*You* don't want to do anything spontaneous."

"I'm a planner, true." Alex couldn't argue the point. That was why he was asking now instead of waiting.

Phil nodded. "There are things coming up. The Bit and Spur is throwing a holiday dance in the community center. Ladies are getting all dolled up in dresses and such. Guys are talking about suits. Which will be a trick with this thing. But Declan's got a live band coming up for it, weather permitting. If not, Dillon Bradshaw will play DJ. I was planning on taking Sarah, and the girls are already booked for babysitting." The girls were twelve and fourteen, as Alex found out during one of their dinners, but they acted older.

Phil scratched his chin. "The Hollisters are funding the decorations, and the townsfolk are going to put up the Christmas doodads to make the town look brighter. We're staging at the community hall not this weekend, but next, the lights were delayed getting here. But we'll leave them up a bit past New Year to make up for the delay. You could take her to that. Going to be a great time."

"Thank you, I'll ask her." It was far enough out he could get behind that.

"Glad to hear it. Oh, that same day, we're going to put up a Christmas tree down the road here. The Marshalls will bring that into town and set it up. So there'll be a lighting ceremony after we get all the decorations done. Hot cocoa and such, along with a blessing by both Father Murphey and Reverend Campbell."

"So, a day-long event." He'd never decorated a town before. It could be fun, or it could be a total disaster. Depended on who was running the show.

Phil nodded. "Then there's the bonfire. Right outside of town. We do that the weekend before Christmas if the weather is good. We'll have spiced cider, and the kids will make s'mores. It's nothing but an opportunity to get together and stay warm while we do it. The men have a little something that they spike the cider with, but nobody gets sloppy."

"I rarely drink. The last beer I had was when I got these stitches. The other one you sent over is still in the refrigerator and probably will be there until I leave."

"Mmmm ... I have my one beer a day, Monday through Friday, over at Declan's. I support his business, and I get to visit with the guys who don't make it to the garage. I'm there thirty minutes, and then I head home. Sarah calls it my decompression time. I just like visiting." Phil chuckled. "I hear there's going to be a White Elephant Christmas party at the community hall. I'll get you a date on that. It's supposed to be a potluck dinner, and bring a funny gift that's wrapped up. Not expensive, mind you. Most will recycle the gifts they've received but couldn't use or didn't need."

Alex leaned forward. "Oh, like a Dirty Santa exchange?"

"A what now?" Phil's brow furrowed.

"You draw numbers, and you get to pick the gift that's wrapped and under the tree. They can steal a gift three times. If you take it on the third time, it's yours, and no one can steal it again."

"Huh, well, we draw numbers, but none of that stealing stuff happens."

Alex shrugged. "Just makes it a little more interesting."

"It could indeed." Phil smiled. "I'll talk to

Declan and see what he thinks. Other than that, I have two snowmobiles. You could take her out riding. Horses aren't a good idea this time of year."

"I'm hesitant to ride either a snowmobile or a horse." He patted his leg. "I don't think they could piece me back together again."

"Can I ask what happened?" Phil held up a hand. "If you were on some mission or something, just tell me to mind my own business."

"I wish. I was running the O-course. We have this webbed ladder tower. It's about twenty-five feet tall. I was flying over it, but the webbing at the top snapped. I had a hold of the nylon strapping but nothing else. I tried to grab onto something else, so I didn't fall twenty feet and land on my head. So, I grabbed at the webbing with this hand and was jerked around. My leg went through the square opening of the strapping, and I twisted as I fell, catching myself. I tried to pull out, but my foot slammed back through the webbing just as the guy behind me came over the top and started his rapid descent. The webbing trapped my leg, his body weight, and the way the webbing had me twisted plus the gravity of my own weight collided. I snapped my fibula, shattered my tibia, dislocated my knee, and caused a compound fracture of my femur. I had to be cut from the webbing. I don't remember that part. I'd passed out from the pain."

"Damn, didn't the other guy see you?"

"No. He didn't know I'd got twisted up. When you're running the course, you're focused on the next thing, not the guy in front of you doing what he needs to do. You're expected to be done and gone. Everyone handles their piece, so the team works effectively. Especially in my old career field."

"I take it you weren't a mechanic." Phil cocked his head.

"What gave you that idea? I'm a brilliant mechanic. What are you talking about?" Once again, he deflected. It was ingrained in his DNA.

"Right." Phil chuckled and tried to scratch inside his cast with a pen. "Don't hurt her. She's just lost her mom. You won't see it. It's not like her to show anything but happiness, but losing her momma was hard on her. Not getting into school had to be a blow, too, but she won't talk about it. Not even to Sarah. That's why we figure it meant more than she's letting on."

Alex rolled his eyes and chuckled. "Phil, I'm not asking for permission to date her, but I get and appreciate the protective stance."

"We're all the family she has left, so I'm acting as a stand-in for her dad. God rest his soul."

Alex nodded. "I get it. But here's the thing, I like her. She's got a magnetic field around her, and yeah, I'm attracted to her. But I'm not an ass. I'm not a user. I was raised by a man who respected women and, in turn, taught me to respect them. I would never intentionally hurt her."

"Well, that's aboveboard and honest. I can accept that." Phil pointed to the computer. "Do you want me to print you out a calendar so you can put those things down?"

Alex chuckled and pulled out his phone. "Nah, I'll use this."

"Get 'em scheduled and then hang onto your hat, son. That girl is a whirling dervish in the best way possible."

Alex pointed to his forehead. "I could have used that warning before she showed up."

Phil belted out a laugh. "Ah, hell, son. Where's the fun in that?"

Alex waited until Phil was done with his henpecking, and then they closed up shop. When he stepped outside, the sky was clear, although it was dark. The stars twinkled in a massive array of beauty. "Damn, would you look at that?"

Phil looked up with him. "Don't get that in the cities, do you?"

"No, sir, we do not." Alex stared at the multitude. "That's amazing."

"Add stargazing to your list of things to do. Sometimes it's nice enough." Phil slapped him in the gut.

Alex grunted although the tap didn't hurt. Phil chuckled. "I'm going to go have my beer. See you tomorrow."

Alex glanced back up at the stars. "Yep. Tomorrow."

Getting into his truck, he let it warm up before making his way back to the cabin. A smile crossed his face when he saw Phil's old truck still parked there. He parked and plugged the truck in, just in case the temperatures dropped again. Then he walked up the stairs and into the cabin. The smell of something delicious hit him just before he opened the door. And as he walked in, he drooled at the aroma.

"Hi! I'm just about ready to leave." Kayla stood with her coat in her hand.

"What did you make?"

"Oh, I stopped over at Gens before lunch and got a frozen dinner. I'm not much of a cook myself. I wanted to do something nice for you since you're letting me use your cabin. I won't stay this late again." She put her arm through her coat.

"Is there enough for both of us?" He took his coat off after taking off his gloves.

Kayla put her hands on her hips. "I think so, but I saw how much you ate at breakfast, so … maybe not?"

Alex laughed. "Stay and have dinner with me. We can visit without an audience." He was still a bit miffed at the welcoming committee that morning. Not that he could blame the guys; they were being hospitable. *Yeah, right.*

"Thank you, let me see if Aunt Sarah needs the truck for anything first."

"Phil will be home in …" He glanced at his watch. "Twenty-five minutes. Which reminds me, we changed the tire on your SUV and ran a diagnostic check. There was nothing wrong."

She stopped taking off her coat. "But it wouldn't start."

"I know. It wouldn't start for us either. Some wires from the wiring harness were worn, and it looks like it shorted out."

"What is there to short out?"

"The electrical computer system that runs your

truck. We changed all the fuses, repaired the wires, and she started right up. Phil wants to order you a new tire, your spare. The tire is almost bald, which will rupture sooner rather than later. It should be here by Thursday." Alex looked at his hands. "I'm going to go wash up."

"So, I can drive us to Rapid on Friday?"

"Yep," he called back as he walked into the bathroom. He used a pumice soap to clean the grease from his hands.

Kayla placed another dinner setting on the table while he washed. "Thank you again for dinner," he said as he came back in. While he poured them both water, she grabbed two hot pads and lifted a pan out of the oven. "Man, that smells good." He rubbed his hands together and sat down.

"Shepherd's pie." She smiled. "There's fresh bread on the counter. Could you grab it?"

"Done." He snatched the cutting board and the small loaf of bread and placed them on the counter that served as his dinner table. Before he sat down, he retrieved the butter.

Kayla served them, and the food tasted just as good as the smell had advertised. "So, you wanted to visit?" She lifted a forkful of food. "About what?"

He swallowed what was in his mouth. "How old are you?"

She chuckled and pointed her fork at him. "You aren't supposed to ask a lady that."

"Sorry, not sorry." He laughed when she stuck her tongue out at him.

"I'm twenty-eight. How old are you?"

"Thirty-five." He shook his head. "I thought for sure I'd retire from the Army and start my second career around forty. The obstacle course had different ideas."

"Is that where you hurt your leg?"

"Destroyed it is more the correct term. And yes." He described what happened.

"Oh, dear heavens above. I'm so sorry."

Alex shrugged. "Believe me, I was angry. I went through the entire process, the surgeries, the rehab, more surgeries with the determination to get back to one hundred percent. After eighteen months, the Army said they'd done all they could do, and I was no longer qualified to do the job I was assigned."

"What was that?" She took a bite of her bread.

He drew a deep breath. "Special Forces. I can't say much more than that."

She nodded. "Like the Navy SEALs?"

Alex rolled his eyes. "Kind of like that." *Better and less known, but kind of like that.*

"Couldn't you have worked as a mechanic in the Army?"

He put his fork down and reflected before he spoke. "I love being a mechanic. I'm good at it. But what I did in the Army was at such a level that going back to the regular grunt duties would be depressing. Plus, the Army would have to give me a permanent profile because of the leg, so I opted for medical retirement."

"Retirement?"

"Yes. My rank and the years I served were calculated, and the government gives me a monthly retirement check."

"Oh, so that's it." She smiled. "You were very nice to work for Uncle Phil for twenty-five percent. Just about every night at dinner, Phil mentions how you were sent to Hollister by an angel."

Alex snorted. "Not an angel. A woo-woo woman, maybe." He stopped and then frowned. "Well, she could be an angel. I'm not an authority on that type of thing."

Kayla set her fork down and leaned forward.

"You do know I didn't understand a word you just said, right?"

He chuckled. "There was this woman at the Atlanta airport. My flight had been delayed, then canceled, then un-canceled. Anyway, while I was there, she suggested I try a bit of spontaneity. She said something to the effect that it would lead to good things."

Kayla scooped him another serving out of the pan. "You said you were trying to be more ... agile with your schedule. Is that the reason?"

He cut another slice of bread as he answered, "It is. When Nail, the friend I was helping in Rapid City, got the call from Phil, he suggested I come up here. Normally, I would have said no, thank you. But I agreed to come up and meet Phil. I figured he if didn't have a good shop, I'd decline."

"He has a really nice one now. For a long time, he worked out of those two little bays in the front part." Kayla took another bite of her dinner. "He got some money and invested it in the business and put some away for each of the girls for college."

"Smart. He has an excellent reputation around here. At least as far as being a mechanic is concerned."

Kayla's eyes popped up to stare at him. "What?"

Alex chuckled and held up a finger as he chewed the bite he'd just shoved into his mouth. "Seems your uncle Phil has a reputation for knowing everything about everyone."

"Oh." She laughed, and Alex watched her relax. "Well, he is a bit of a social butterfly."

"A bit," Alex agreed. "What about you? Tell me about Kayla Bryce."

She leaned back in her chair. "Well, I'm an Air Force brat. My mom met Dad down in Rapid City. It was his first duty assignment, and they fell in love and got married. Mom followed him overseas and then back to stateside assignments. I was born, and they sent Dad on a remote assignment where we couldn't go with him. After that, we pretty much stayed at Hill Air Force Base. Dad was an engineer, and he worked with some of the development things going on there. He died one morning. Mom said he complained of a wicked headache that morning. But he got ready for work, finished breakfast, kissed my mom, told her he loved her, kissed me, and told me to be good for my mom. He walked three steps and went down. We called 911, but he didn't make it. A brain aneurysm. The doctors said he had a subarachnoid hemorrhage that caused his death."

She smiled at him, the exact opposite of what he'd thought she'd do. "How many people get to say goodbye? He did. Both Mom and I told him we loved him. After all the grief and heartache, we decided that would be our constant in our memories of Dad. He knew, and we knew, how much love was in our house."

Alex reached across the table and took her hand. "That's a beautiful way to remember him."

She nodded. "Mom and I were pretty much inseparable until college. They diagnosed her with Parkinson's disease just before I was about to complete my degree. So, I left school, and Mom and I made a list of things she wanted to do before she became incapacitated, and we did them. We spent most of the money Dad left us seeing the world and having wonderful experiences. When Mom couldn't go any longer, we talked about what we'd done. What we'd seen. Toward the end, I talked for both of us. We were blessed to have that time together. When she passed, she left me a small amount of money and a heart filled with memories."

Alex held her hand and squeezed it a bit. "What about college? Did you want to finish?"

"Oh, I did. Online courses when my mom was homebound. I even applied for a design school I'd once been interested in attending." She laughed and shook her head but kept her hand in his. "I submitted some designs I loved and had worked on for years. They weren't well received." She lowered her eyes. "But I know everything happens for a reason." She looked up at him again and smiled. "I believe that. You better finish before it gets cold." She nodded to his food, and he reluctantly released her warm hand. "What do your mom and dad think of you coming to South Dakota to work?"

Alex lifted his shoulders. "I never knew my mom. She and my dad weren't married, and she didn't hang around long after I was born. Dad never said a bad word about her, though. He said she'd given me life, and for that, he'd always love her. He passed when I was in the service. I found out too late that he'd run into a hard patch and had taken loans out against his business. By the time I settled all the debt, I only had his personal tools and the memories of the greatest father in the world."

Kayla smiled at him. "So, you're all alone, too?"

He nodded but added, "You have your aunt and uncle."

"I do." She smiled. "I'm lucky."

They ate in silence for a while before he asked, "Did you ever tell Edna you were going to work here?"

"Oh, yes. Today. I went over to the community hall and met Melody, her boys, and Declan, her husband. They're really nice people."

"I've met Declan." He nodded.

"I'm going to teach a class on Thursday nights. Not Wednesday. That's reserved for the Winchesters."

Alex stopped with his water glass halfway to his mouth. "I have no idea what that means."

"Me either, but it isn't to be messed with, according to Edna and Melody. So, Thursdays it is. This Thursday, I'm going to give them an overview of what quilting entails. A project can take a long time, but if you have a group of people to help, it can go quicker. I think these ladies want a social circle as much as they want to learn how to quilt." Kayla laughed. "I'll help them with that. Oh!" She jumped off the chair, jogged to her coat, and retrieved her phone. "I worked on this today."

She came back and gave him the phone. The note app was up, and he read through her thoughts. He looked up at her. "This could work here. The consignment shop, having a few stock items, and the tailor shop. This is a great business idea."

She smiled wide. "Right? But the long pole in the tent is the location. I want to poke around, but I don't want to tell Uncle Phil and Aunt Sarah in case it doesn't happen. I know they'd want to help, but this is something I need to do on my own."

Alex cocked his head. "Why is that?"

She put her phone on the table. "I'm twenty-eight. I need to stand on my own two feet. If this works out, it'll be because I made it work. And I will do that, you know. I'll make it work. I just need a location."

Alex stared at her for a moment. "I have no doubt you'll do anything you set out to do." He reached for her hand and pulled her closer to him. "I'm going to kiss you now."

Kayla leaned toward him. "All talk and no action."

Alex smiled as he lowered his mouth to hers. He teased his lips against hers and then licked her lips. She yielded to him, and the attraction that surrounded the woman exploded into a reaction that caused both of them to pull away. He stared down into her eyes.

"Don't stop." She breathed the words.

He had no intention of stopping. Alex coaxed and teased her into a dance that consumed the air between them. He pulled away slowly, dropping to kiss her once, twice more. "Wow." She breathed the word with her eyes closed. When she opened them, those beautiful hazel eyes were just as spellbound as he felt.

"I agree." He pushed her hair back and cupped her cheek. "You should go home."

"Should I?" she asked, staring up at him.

"I need to be a gentleman."

"You do?"

He smiled and dropped to kiss her again. "Tonight, yes."

"Tomorrow night?"

"More of this."

"Okay." She backed away from him and smiled. "I'll see you for breakfast."

"I'll be waiting." She took her coat off the peg, and Alex took it from her, holding it for her to put on. She turned around, and he grabbed the collar of the coat, holding her gently. "One for the road."

"Oh, definitely. The road needs one." She lifted her arms to circle his neck. Alex dropped to kiss her. Fuck, the taste of her was beyond exquisite. It was as if magic had combined all the best experiences in the universe and blended them, pouring the essence into her so he could sample the pure taste of heaven.

Pulling away from her was harder than he thought it would be. Yet he somehow managed. "Tomorrow."

She nodded and turned, almost running into the door. He reached around her and opened it. She walked out and down the steps, and he watched as she got into the truck and started it up. Then, walking out to the end of the porch, he watched her drive away. When he could no longer see her taillights, he looked up at the multitude of stars and realized South Dakota had gotten under his skin. He suddenly understood why people wanted to live in Hollister. The desolate beauty, the people, and the culture combined and created heaven on earth.

CHAPTER 13

Kayla pulled up in front of her aunt and uncle's home. She'd floated home. The tires on the truck hadn't touched the street. Her icy fingers touched her lips, but even the chill of a South Dakota winter couldn't quench the burn of the heat they'd shared. She closed her eyes and dropped back into the seat. It jumbled her insides with excitement and long, long dormant sensations.

She jumped when the passenger side door opened. "Aunt Sarah!" Kayla held her hand to her chest. "You scared me."

"Well, you've been out here for a while. I thought I'd check on you." She sat down and shut the door after her. "What's up?"

"Nothing, really. Just ..." Kayla turned to face her aunt. "Alex Thompson and I are dating."

Sarah blinked at her. "That's ... Well, isn't that a little fast?"

Kayla laughed. "It is, but it also feels so right. I've had no one of the male persuasion in my life for so long. I'm enjoying his companionship." She was also enjoying the kissing and, hopefully, a lot more physical contact, but her aunt didn't need to know that.

"Well, he's a good man, but guard your heart." Sarah glanced around. "He's great looking, too. That close shaved beard and mustache." Her aunt fanned herself.

"Aunt Sarah!" Kayla laughed hard as her aunt smiled widely.

"What? I'm married, not dead. I notice things."

"Uncle Phil would have a cow!"

"What? You think he doesn't look at the girls at the bar? I don't mind if he gets thirsty there, as long as he drinks at home, if you know what I mean."

Kayla's mouth dropped open. "I ... I ... have no idea what to say to that."

Sarah laughed. "Girl, if your momma didn't tell

you that women and men still get together after children, she should have."

Kayla barked out a surprised laugh. "Aunt Sarah, I've never seen this side of you."

Sarah smiled. "You've been here a handful of times, and you were so worried about your momma. It wasn't appropriate to have fun and tease then. It is now. You're a grown woman. What you do with your life is your choice. Alex, in my opinion, is a good choice. Now, let's stop wasting gas and go inside. I saved you some dinner."

"Thank you. I'll take it for lunch tomorrow. I ate with Alex. Oh, Aunt Sarah, you should see the clothes that I'm making for the girls." Kayla turned off the engine. "I'll sneak them home to wrap them while the girls are at school so I can show you."

They both got out of the truck and headed to the house. "Don't you work too hard now. This is a vacation for you, and Edna told me you're teaching starting Thursday."

"I am, and I'm looking forward to it. I have a feeling some of the ladies will drop out when they find out how involved it is."

"Probably, or they might keep coming just to have something to do on Thursday nights that doesn't involve pots, pans, or laundry." Sarah opened the door.

"What were you two doing outside?" Uncle Phil grumbled as he slowly poured himself a cup of coffee with his left hand.

"Girl talk," Sarah said as she took off her coat. "We'd tell you, but then you'd have to suffer through all the hen meetings you'd be included in."

"Bah … I get all the information I need from the source." Her uncle winked at her. "Did you enjoy yourself tonight?"

Sarah put her hands on her hips. "He told you?"

"Asked for things to do around Hollister. Our young niece here is fixing on being courted."

"Courted?" Kayla looked from her uncle to her aunt. "No one says that anymore."

"Well, around here, they do. Sarah, your show's about to start." Phil picked up his coffee. "I also warned him not to hurt you."

Kayla palmed her face with both hands. "Why would you do that? Seriously, that didn't happen, did it?"

"Darn straight it did." Phil glanced out to where the girls were doing their homework. "Any lady needs someone to make sure they're treated right."

"Dad, that is so old-fashioned. You know we can speak for ourselves, right?" Kimber, Phil's oldest daughter, said.

"And if they don't listen, we know how to defend ourselves," Carol, the younger one, added.

"Remember, Dad, we know what happens to bulls to make them steers. Couldn't be too much different," Kimber agreed.

Kayla felt her eyes widen as she peeked around the corner. "Okay, I'm officially terrified of both of you." The girls laughed, and Phil grunted something before he headed to the living room to watch television. "Seriously, y'all scare me." Kayla tossed Carol's hair on the way through the small dining room where the girls were working.

"Kayla, are you dating Alex?" Kimber asked as she followed Kayla into the hallway.

Kayla turned around at the doorway of the guest bedroom. "I am. Why?"

Kimber shrugged her shoulders. "I like him." She pushed her long brown hair out of her face. "Not *like* like him, because I know he's way too old for me, but he's nice, you know. Some of the guys at school are just jerks."

Kayla leaned against the wall. "Teenage boys

are … unique. Wait until you go to college. The world opens up."

Kimber looked behind her and then looked back before whispering, "Did you date in high school?"

Kayla stepped closer to her cousin. "I had a couple of dates. They weren't anything to write home about. Mostly guys wanting to brag that they did things that did not happen."

Kimber sighed. "There's this one boy. Clay Thompson. He and his family moved into the area last winter. Clay is older. He just turned nineteen, but Miss Prentiss accepted him into the homeschool program the town uses so he could get his high school diploma. He's really smart, and he asked me to go to the bonfire with him."

Kayla smiled, but she was cautious. The age gap was big for a young lady like Kimber. "Did you tell your mom?"

"No, she wouldn't understand." Kimber sighed.

Kayla beckoned her closer by crooking her finger. Kimber leaned in. "I'm going to let you in on a little secret. Your mom is a thousand percent cooler than you give her credit for. Talk to her. I promise she'll understand."

Kimber stared at her. "Do you think so?"

"I do. Talk to her. If she says no, you'll have a reason. If she says yes, but has conditions, you need to listen and obey those rules. At nineteen, he's considered an adult, so I think your parents would be very concerned. But not telling them would be a huge mistake."

"Okay. Thanks, Kayla."

"No problem." She watched Kimber head back to the dining room. "Hey, twerp."

Kimber turned around, and Kayla made a face. "You two really do scare me with your talk about bulls and steers."

Kimber laughed and headed into the dining room. Kayla smiled and let herself into her room. She leaned against the door and closed her eyes. When her phone vibrated in her pocket, she took it out and squinted at the bright light in the darkness of her room.

>> Thank you again for dinner.

Kayla took off her coat and flopped onto the bed. She rolled over and texted.

>>>Thank you for dessert.

She watched the bubbles on the messenger app dance, then stop. They danced a bit more and then stopped. She typed again.

>>>Did I embarrass you?

Kayla watched the bubbles again.

>>No, I'm not shy, and I don't get embarrassed easily. I was trying to figure out a way to say that you are exceptionally sexy. But I don't want you to think I want to date you just for sex.

Kayla bit her bottom lip and tapped at the screen.

>>>Darn. I'm actually just dating you for the sex.

She snorted to herself and kept typing.

>>> Joking, but I do understand what you mean. There is chemistry.

>> Explosive chemistry.

>>>Complaining?

>> Not for a second. Sleep well. I'll see you in the morning.

>>> Good night.

She put the phone down and flopped face-first into the bedding. A laugh bubbled up. She was texting with a man she really liked. When had her life flip-flopped? Kayla rolled over onto her back and closed her eyes. She didn't care. She liked him and enjoyed his company. The kisses tonight were easily an eight-point-nine on the Richter scale. They tumbled her insides into a mess of sensations. The result shattered her ideas of having a few dates and then packing up and leaving.

She opened her eyes and stared up at the ceiling. "I think you'd like him, Momma."

CHAPTER 14

Alex tossed his book onto the coffee table. It was amazing how quickly he'd lost interest in the story now that Kayla was in his life. Tonight, however, she was teaching her quilting lesson, but she'd promised to swing by before returning to Phil and Sarah's place. They'd had breakfast every morning, and thankfully, the single men in the area got the word that they were dating. Sure, they ribbed the hell out of him at lunch and when they stopped by the garage, but that didn't matter at all. He had thick enough skin, and they were never disrespectful to Kayla in the verbal jabs. It was like he was back in the military. Seemed the unit known as Hollister had accepted the new guy, and he was fair game, like everyone else. He was okay with that. He liked the town, even though everyone seemed to know a bit too much about everyone else, but that was what made the town special.

He and Kayla had spent every evening together, too. When the kisses got too intense, they walked out in the cold and looked at the brilliance of the stars. He'd dated women before. He wasn't a monk. But he wasn't a manwhore like a couple of the guys in his unit. In order to spend time with a woman, there had to be more than just an attraction. His dad had taught him that. *"If you don't like the lady you're with, Alex, you won't respect her. That's what's wrong with relationships today. You need to be friends, then lovers. Not the other way around."*

"Were you Mom's friend?"

"Yes, we were great friends, but she was young and afraid of many things."

"Afraid of me?"

"No." His dad put his arm around his shoulders. *"She was like a wild bird. Flittering here and there. She didn't want to land. I don't think she ever will. But for a short time, we were together, and she gave me you. I will always love her for that."*

Alex turned the memories over in his mind. He

wondered if his mother ever thought about him. He rarely thought about her unless, like tonight, his memories were aided by thoughts of his father.

His thoughts moved back to Kayla. She was a bundle of energy and sunshine. Alex chuckled to himself. She was so animated that it made everyone else seem dull in comparison. The charm that radiated from her ensnared men and women alike. To top it off, she was nice. As her uncle said, she'd give someone her last dollar and be happy that she'd been able to help. It was a selflessness he'd rarely seen. Kayla lived it. She wasn't fake or trying to impress anyone; she was just that giving.

They'd gone to the diner that morning, and she'd taken a bag of sewing she'd done for Ciera. Ciera didn't know it, but at the very bottom was a shirt she'd made for Cody, Ciera's son. They'd visited the night before when Kayla finished the shirt. It was made of suede, and Kayla had hand sewn a beautiful picture of a horse's head on the back, along with yoke piping on the front and back. She'd explained that she'd seen the applique and the shirt while in Belle Fourche.

His phone rang, startling him. He picked it up and smiled. "Hey, man, what's up?"

"Still coming down tomorrow night?" Nail asked.

"I am. Bringing a friend. She'll stay at a hotel, though. I'll bunk with you, if that's cool?"

"Sure ... so, she's not *that* kind of friend?" Nail emphasized the word and then laughed.

"She could be. Someday, but I'm not pushing the issue." Alex put his feet up on the coffee table and relaxed back on the couch.

"Oh, damn. I was joking. Who is she? Would I know her? Allison?"

"From the little market? Nope. Her name is Kayla, the one who brained me and gave me a concussion. You know, I told you about her. She's Phil's niece."

There was silence on the other end of the line. Alex looked at the phone. There was still a connection. "Hey, you still there?"

Nail cleared his throat. "Dude, you never told me who that chick was. Just that she was hot. Just how old is this *girl*?"

Alex frowned. "The *woman* is twenty-eight. Why?"

Nail let out a whoosh of air and spoke quickly, "Fuck, man, I know how young Phil's girls are, and you said niece, so I was thinking..."

Alex sat up and yelled into the phone, "That I would ever be interested in jailbait? Thanks, man. You fucking know me better than that, or I hoped you did."

"I'm sorry, dude. I just couldn't put two and two together," Nail apologized. "That's why I was stunned into silence."

"Right." Alex snorted. Nail was never at a loss for words. Having stunned him was probably a tremendous accomplishment. But damn it. It stung that his friend would think, even for a second, he'd do something so out of character.

"Dude, I apologized. What do you want, a dozen roses?"

"Yes and chocolates." Alex rolled his eyes. "Asshole."

"I am. One hundred percent. I'll get your flowers and chocolates because that was my bad. What time will you be down tomorrow night?"

"Late. We're leaving after I finish work. I'm taking her out to dinner, then to her hotel. She's going to object, but I want to make sure she's safe behind a dead-bolted door. I'll drive her vehicle over and then return in the morning, so she has her car."

"My old junker not good enough for you?" Nail chuckled.

"Nah, she runs like a champ, but Kayla wants to drive around to different stores and such while I'm working. I'll bring her over in the morning to introduce you."

"Do that, and, dude, I'm happy you found someone."

"On that topic, why did Allison's name pop out of your mouth so quickly?" Alex had his suspicions.

"Don't go there."

"Why?"

"She's the deputy sheriff's woman."

"No, she isn't."

"What are you talking about?" Nail shot the words out quicker than he'd expected.

"Ken and I wind up at the diner every morning at about the same time or at least eat lunch together on the daily. I've gotten to know him pretty well. He mentioned Allison shot him down for the last time. They haven't dated since high school or something like that. As far as I know, Allison isn't attached to anyone." Ken was a damn good guy. He'd told Alex what had happened and when. Allison seemed to be a bit ... spiteful ...

maybe ... about a thing that happened when they were still kids. But that wasn't his worry.

Nail cleared his throat, a habit he had when he was nervous. "You're not joking, are you?"

"No. I wouldn't do that. Come up for a weekend and see. Better yet, a couple of events are coming up where the whole town will be involved. You should drive up for one of them."

Nail drew a deep breath. "I don't know. Maybe. I've got my hands full here, but I did like talking with her. She's straightforward. No bullshit, no hedging. My type of woman."

"Then consider driving up. I have the dates on my phone. I'll give them to you when I come down. You have an open invite."

"As I said, I'll think about it. If it gets too late Friday night and I need to sack out, I'll leave the back door open and the light on for you."

"That works. I'll see you tomorrow."

Alex disconnected, knowing Nail wouldn't say goodbye. He sat back and relaxed. He couldn't believe Nail. The man was an idiot at times, but he was a service brother and a damn good friend. A pair of headlights through the window grabbed his attention. Kayla was pulling up. The tire had arrived that morning, and he'd replaced it first thing and then driven her back to Phil's, dropping off Phil's old truck so she could drive her SUV. He stepped outside. The night was still and so cold the air stole a person's breath. But the woman who stepped out of the truck did a better job at leaving him breathless.

"Hi, how did it go?" He grabbed her hand as she walked up the stairs, and they went into the cabin together.

"I didn't know there were that many ladies in this part of the world. I had at least …" She shook her head. "Forty ladies there. It was amazing."

He helped her take off her coat and smiled at the fluffy pink sweater that followed her curves and accentuated her waist. He hung up the coat and pulled her into his arms. "Do you think all of them will be back?"

She beamed up at him. "No. I think this was more social than anything, but the serious ones came up after I finished and asked specific questions about what types of items to buy. I think that group is about fifteen strong. Oh! I figured out what Winchester Wednesday is."

He laughed. "Do tell."

"It's a program they watch every Wednesday night. *Supernatural*. Anyway, they stream it.

They're on the third time through the series, and it has hundreds of episodes. But they have wine and visit. They invited me to come out and watch but warned me I'd need a ride home or to stay the night. The ladies at the Marshall ranch are so funny and nice." She bounced a bit on her toes. "I really hope I can find a place to set up shop here in Hollister. There's so much to like about this little town."

Alex smiled down at her. "I only needed one thing to know I liked this town." He pulled her toward him.

Her voice lowered, and she purred, "Really? What was that?"

"You." He covered her lips with his. Her scent was intoxicating. Her kisses blurred reality, making him forget the world outside their embrace. His hand traveled to her breast, and he rubbed her nipple through the material of her shirt and bra. She groaned and pushed into his very interested cock. "God, I want you."

She entwined her arms around his neck, and her fingers played with his hair. She leaned back and looked up at him. "What's stopping you?"

"Decorum." He buried his head at her neck and licked his way to her ear. "When we make this happen, I'm not letting you out of my bed. The entire town would know you spent the night with me. I'm protecting your reputation."

"Screw decorum." She moaned and tipped her head so he could access more skin. "I have a hotel in Rapid this weekend. No one would know." She placed her hands on either side of his head and made him stop and look at her. "No one would know. Two nights away from here."

Alex stared at her. "Are you sure?"

"I'm a woman. I know my own mind, and I know what I want." She toed up and kissed him.

He got on board with the kiss and devoured her. The thought of having her naked under him… He broke the kiss and drew a deep breath. He needed to cool things down a bit, or he'd be busting a nut in his jeans like some horny teenager at a freshman dance. "I don't want you to regret this. Us."

She blinked as if rebooting her mind and then smiled. "Why would I?"

Alex stared at her. "I'm a temporary fix here, remember?"

Kayla's expression fell. She stared up at him for a moment, and then that radiant smile reappeared. "No one knows what the future holds. I may leave, too. My dreams are just that, at the moment. I'm not willing to let this thing between us go without ever knowing you."

"Neither am I. Tomorrow night."

Kayla toed up again. "It's a date."

CHAPTER 15

Kayla pulled up in front of the cabin, but before she could get out of her SUV, Alex was out the door and heading her way. He opened the door, swooped down, and kissed the breath from her lungs. "Wow, good morning." She inhaled the scent of the man, and it was magnificent.

"Good morning. I'll go with you today, and we can leave the truck here. Just a second." He trotted back to the cabin and reached inside, grabbing a duffle bag. Then he made a beeline to the passenger side and tossed the bag in the back. "This way, we can leave from the station." He leaned over and kissed her again. "Better shut the door."

Kayla blinked and then laughed. "Who are you, and what have you done with Alex?"

He did a double-take at her. "What do you mean?"

"My Alex likes to stick to his schedule. Who are you?"

He drew a breath and rolled his eyes up to the top of the vehicle. "Hmm ... a man who wants to be alone with a woman he desires. That has loosened a bit of my phobia about my schedule."

She chuckled and put the crossover into reverse. "I don't think you have a phobia."

"Probably not, but I don't do spur-of-the-moment well. I had all last night to think about today, so I had a little advance warning."

"Did you sleep well?" She batted her eyes at him as she pulled onto the main road through town.

"Not a wink. You?"

"Maybe on and off an hour or so." She laughed. "We're like teenagers planning for sex on prom night."

Alex barked out a laugh. "That's the truth." When she parked, he hopped out and walked around to open her door. He always opened doors for her, which was something she noticed men around here routinely did. It was nice, and it wasn't condescending in the slightest. Some of the women she'd gone to college with detested it when men opened the door or pulled out a chair for them. Frankly, Kayla had never seen the issue with anyone being polite. Besides, when Alex opened the door for her, put his hand on her back, or any of the other many tiny things he did, it made her feel special, and that was so uplifting.

They took off their coats in the diner and hung them on the pegs on the wall by the door. While Kayla took a seat, Alex got them coffee from the cart. He added cream and sugar to both of them. They were the only ones in the diner that morning.

"Morning!" Gen walked out of the kitchen. "Ciera has the day off. If I remember correctly, you're a sausage biscuit?" She pointed to Alex.

Alex shook his head and politely corrected her. "No, ma'am. Ham, please, and a glass of milk."

"Ham and a milk. That's right. Got it. What about you, Kayla?" She'd met Gen again at the quilting class last night, although she'd seen her at the diner on the last trip to Hollister that her mother was able to make.

"I'll just have a bit of his biscuit and coffee, thanks."

"Okay, I'll bring you out the biggest biscuit I have back there so you can share." Gen stopped about halfway to the kitchen. "I went home last night and looked up patterns. I have one I'd like to do, but I'm thinking I may be biting off more than I can chew." She screwed up her face into a grimace.

Kayla laughed and waved her hand. "Pick the one you like. We'll make it happen."

Gen clapped her hands together. "I was hoping you'd say that." She spun and headed back into the kitchen.

Alex draped his arm over her shoulders, and she settled in beside him as she spoke. "I really had a good time last night. The ladies are so wonderful." She leaned into him. "But I'm really looking forward to going to Rapid tonight."

Alex lifted his eyebrows and took a sip of his coffee. "So am I."

The door jingled, and Kayla leaned forward past Alex to see who'd come into the diner. A man she hadn't seen before stood in the doorway. "Do you know who runs the gas station or what time they'll open?"

Alex nodded. "I work there."

"I'm about out of gas. Do you think you could open early?"

"Sure." He took another sip of his coffee and winked at her. "I'll be right back."

Kayla watched as they left and then moved to the other side of the booth so she could watch the men. "Where did he go?" Gen asked when she came back with the biscuit and milk.

"Someone was close to running out of gas, so Alex went to open the pumps for him." She pointed out the window.

"Huh, I don't recognize the guy." Gen put the food and milk down and stood beside her.

Something's wrong. Kayla couldn't tell what, but Alex's body language was off. He pumped the gas and lifted the plastic that covered whatever was in the back. Alex said something to the man. The stranger flicked the plastic back into place, shoved some money at Alex, and got in the truck. Alex barely got the gas cap on the tank before the man left.

"Well, that was ... odd," Gen said what she was thinking.

"I wonder what he saw." Kayla stared at the truck, a nondescript blue Ford that looked like a hundred others in the area.

She watched as Alex locked up the station and headed back. "I'll get him a fresh coffee."

"He likes cream and sugar, two of each, please," Kayla said as she switched back to their side of the booth.

Alex came in and took off his coat. "What was that guy's problem?" Gen asked as she handed him the hot coffee.

"Thank you. I'm not sure. He was transporting a custom-made bike. It was lying on its side. Beautiful purple with silver flames that disappeared and reappeared as you looked at it. I asked him where he bought the bike. He told me to mind my own business, shoved a fifty in my hand, and took off." Alex's brow furrowed. "Something about the guy made me cautious."

"Well, at least he's gone," Gen said and dropped a hand on his shoulder. "Good riddance, too. Let me know if you two need anything else."

Kayla thanked her and waited until she'd gone back to the kitchen. "Something's bothering you about this, the same way it bothered you about the other motorcycle. The one the night you came and defrosted me."

Alex glanced at her and smiled. "It just seems to me that transporting custom bikes in the dead of winter is strange. Laying one down on its side like that is wrong. Where are they going? Why aren't they protecting the paint jobs on those bikes? If they can afford a custom, can't they afford the proper tie-down straps and a cover? Better yet, a trailer. It doesn't make sense. Some of those bikes can go for six figures, especially the really old, restored bikes. These were custom. Built from scratch, like Nail builds them. It's irresponsible to transport them like that." He shrugged and shook his head. "But the bikes aren't my property."

She nodded and took a small bite of the biscuit he'd cut for her before she stated, "But it bothers you."

"It does." Alex took a bite of his breakfast. A moment later, he shook his head. "I just can't shake the feeling."

"Is there anything you can do about it?" Kayla asked before sipping her coffee.

"No, and I guess that's what's digging at me. Nail takes such care in building those bikes. He's making one now that will be gorgeous. It isn't a commissioned project, so he'll sell it at the shop. I already told him I'd be willing to buy it. But that build is a side project, and he only works on it when he has time. With his dad out of the office and Nail doing both the admin and the mechanical work, he's swamped."

"Which is why you're going down to help him this weekend." That Alex would give up his free time to help a friend after working all week was a testament to his character.

"He'd do it for me. Besides, it isn't exactly torture to work on the bikes." He looked down at her and lowered his voice. "Leaving you in the morning will be."

A full-body shiver ran through her, and goose flesh popped up on her arms. "I can't wait." Her breathless response was all she could manage. The past week had been heaven and hell. Alex's touch did things to her body that no one had ever done. She *ached* with need. Leaving him and going back to her aunt and uncle's had become harder and harder with each passing evening she spent in his company. Not only because of her desire for sex, which was at an all-time high, but also because she enjoyed his company. They liked the same music, the same types of books, they hadn't talked politics, and that was perfectly fine as far as she was concerned.

"What time do you want me to pick you up?" She was hoping for, say, an hour from now.

"Five. I'll leave when Phil goes to have his beer."

"All right."

"What are you going to do today?"

"I'm finishing a couple of shirts I made for Carol. I finished Kimber's yesterday. Then I want to go through what I brought with me as far as quilting supplies. I'll make a list of what I need so I don't impulse buy." She laughed. "When it comes to fabrics, I'm like a kid in a candy shop."

"I'm that way, too."

"Hardware stores?"

He shook his head.

She guessed again, "Part stores."

"Nope."

"Okay, I give. What store is your shopping weakness?"

"Bookstores. Either the big box store type or the indie-operated ones. They usually have a stock of books from local authors, which is cool." He lifted his coffee cup. "I can spend an entire day in a bookstore. But I don't get the chance to restock very often here."

"I love books, too. I've never spent much time in bookstores, though. But while you're here, you could get an e-reader."

"I've never seen one except in advertisements. I

know some of the guys used to read on their phones, but I've never done that. Mostly because when I was deployed, reading for pleasure wasn't an option. When I was back at base, bookstores were available." He shrugged.

The door opened again, and Edna Michaelson stepped in. Alex's eyes rounded. "That's my cue to leave."

Kayla laughed. They'd discussed Edna's fixation with knowing everything there was to know about Alex. He bent down, kissed her quickly on the lips, and headed to the door. "Edna." He acknowledged her as he grabbed his coat. The woman blinked, her mouth open to say something as he headed out the door, put on his coat, and left.

"Well, where's the fire?"

"He has a lot of work to do today before we head to Rapid for the weekend." Kayla motioned to the booth across from her. "Care to join me?"

"Perfect." Edna filled a cup of coffee and slid into the booth with her. "So, the two of you are going away for a weekend?" Edna's eyes gleamed with mischief.

"No. He's going to his friend's to help him with backed-up work at his motorcycle shop. I'm staying at a hotel and spending the weekend going through all the fabric shops and department stores to find the best bargains I can. Plus, I want to get a few non-homemade things for Christmas." She was going to buy the latest model ear pods for the girls and get Aunt Sarah a new yarn bag and a set of crochet needles. Uncle Phil was the hard one to buy for, but she'd figure something out.

"Oh, well, nothing nefarious, then, darn it." Edna waggled her eyebrows up and down.

Kayla laughed and shook her head. "Nothing. Sorry to disappoint you."

Edna chuckled. "Oh, would you do me a favor? On the way back up, could you stop by the drugstore in Belle? They developed my pictures. I got a text saying so. I have the receipt here." She pulled out her phone and flipped open the case, pulling out the receipt.

"Absolutely." Kayla took it and slid it into her pocket.

"Thank you. That saves me a trip." Edna took a sip of her coffee. "I'm looking forward to next Thursday."

"So am I." Gen came out of the kitchen with a caramel roll for Edna. "Here you go." Gen stood by the booth. "Have you picked out your pattern?" she asked Edna as the woman cut into her roll.

"I have, and I decided for the first one I'd make something just for me. I have boxes full of old clothes I've never had the heart to throw out. Even some of Paul's old shirts. I thought I'd make something with them."

"Paul?" Kayla asked.

"My late husband." Edna cleared her throat. "He passed almost twenty years ago. I put his shirts away. Never threw them out."

"A memory blanket. What a wonderful idea, Edna." Kayla reached across the table and put her hand on the woman's arm. "I'll help you. That's what quilting is all about for me. Memories of working with my mom on them and then, at the end, working on them alone as I talked with her. It's amazing what the simple act of stitching can do for the soul."

"Oh, man. You guys are making me tear up." Gen waved her hands in front of her eyes. "I'm going to go before I start bawling."

Edna cocked her head at Gen's retreating figure.

"What?" Kayla asked when Edna turned back to her.

"She seems kind of emotional lately, doesn't she?"

Kayla looked toward the kitchen and then back at Edna. "I met her for the first time a of couple of years ago and then again last night. If she's emotional, I haven't seen it. I think maybe she was just looking for an excuse to go back to work."

Edna nodded. "Why sure. That's it. You betcha."

Kayla took a sip of her coffee. Somehow, she didn't think Edna really agreed with her.

CHAPTER 16

Alex turned off the interstate heading into Rapid City. Kayla had asked him to drive, and he'd gladly accepted. "So, would you like to stop and get something to eat?"

She looked over at him. "I ... ah ... no."

"What's wrong?" He frowned and glanced over at her. Kayla wasn't hesitant. Ever.

"I thought we were going to the hotel?"

"We are. Aren't you hungry?" He stopped at a stoplight and looked at her. She bit her bottom lip and shook her head slowly from side to side. "Not for food."

A horn honked behind them, and Alex snapped out of his trance. He hit the accelerator and punched the GPS on his phone cradled in the cupholder to the hotel's address. Food had just plummeted to the bottom of any list he'd ever had. They listened to his phone direct them to the hotel, and he pulled up seven minutes later. The longest seven minutes in history.

He grabbed both his duffle and her suitcase out of the back seat, locked the vehicle, and followed her into the hotel lobby. She got the key from the clerk, and they headed to the elevator. "Room three-oh-two." She stepped into the elevator and punched the number three on the control unit. Alex clenched and unclenched his fists on the handles of the cases. The elevator took forever to lift them three flights. He could have raced up and down the stairs ten times, even with his bum leg.

They both saw the arrow pointing toward their room at the same time and turned on a dime. Kayla opened the door after fighting with the keycard to turn the light green. When it finally flickered green, she pushed it open. He walked past her with the luggage and dropped them in a chair wedged in the corner of the small room. Turning, he was not expecting Kayla's launch in his direction. He caught her, and they went over backward. Thankfully, they landed on the bed, and he laughed, shocked and profoundly grateful that his leg hadn't twisted wrong and shut down the night's activities. "Shouldn't we take off our coats?"

She kissed him, stilling his words. His hands found their way under her shirt, and he could feel her wiggling out of her coat. The puffy down material landed on his right. Kayla sat up, staring at him as she stripped off her sweater. Her fall of dark brown hair fell past her shoulders and covered her chest. The light from the bathroom illuminated her pale skin. Her skin was so fair she seemed to shimmer in the faint glow. He placed his hand on her rib cage. They were a stark contrast. His mother was originally from Jamaica, and he'd inherited her skin color. He watched her expression as he let his fingers travel over her body, stopping to cup and tease her breasts through the lace of her bra on the way.

He cupped her neck and pulled her back down to him, running his hands across her back as he kissed her. He found the clasp of her bra and unfastened it, freeing her breasts. Then she shrugged out of the lacy fabric and tossed it somewhere. Alex didn't know where it landed, nor did he care.

Grabbing her around the waist, he rolled and ended up on his knees, suspended over her. She helped him shed his coat. It hit the standing lamp in the room's corner. The lamp fell over the chair, but neither of them cared. Kayla's hands pulled his t-shirt out from his belted jeans, and she ran her fingernails against his rib cage. He shivered in anticipation. While lowering himself, he momentarily froze. Everything he'd imagined doing with this beautiful woman was on the menu, and God help him, he didn't know where to start.

Kayla solved the problem by lifting to kiss him. He kissed her until they were both breathless and then followed his desire. He kissed down her jaw and teased her ear with his tongue. She turned to give him better access and moaned as he moved to her collarbone. So delicate. He kissed, licked, and nipped across it before lowering at a snail's pace to her breasts. She arched under him and grabbed his hair, holding him to her breast. *As if he were leaving anytime soon.*

When he finally dipped lower, he unfastened her jeans while kissing her abdomen. Kayla's legs twisted, and he heard her shoes hit the floor. Easing his body down the bed, Alex pulled the waistband of her jeans and her panties down. He reached for his belt and unfastened it. Kayla lifted to her elbows and watched as he unzipped and stripped out of his jeans, only realizing that he still wore his boots after he'd lowered his jeans.

Kayla laughed as he kicked off the boots, stripped out of his jeans, and crawled up her naked body. He stopped at her knee and licked it. Her leg jerked, so he did the same to the other knee. She spread her legs open, and he took the invitation. Alex moved between her legs and wrapped them in his grip, pulling her closer to his mouth.

She glistened. Damn, he would die right then. He lowered and lightly traced the shape of her core with his tongue. Her body twitched and rocked under him. When he reached the little nub at the top of her sex, he sucked it into his mouth and drove her insane with his tongue and slight pressure from his teeth. She bucked under him. Her hands tried to grip his short hair, finally finding purchase on his shoulders.

"Alex, please." Her fingernails dug into the skin of his shoulders.

He lifted and licked his lips. Her hair splayed across the sheet, her mouth was open, and her lips were full and wet. She arched for him, and he moved, running a hand from her sex to her breast. The expanse of skin was breathtaking and so sexy. She was fucking beautiful in the throes of passion.

He moved up her body. "I need to get a condom." He kissed her and pulled away.

"I'm on the pill. I don't need a condom if you don't."

Alex settled over her again. "Are you sure? I've had so many physicals. I know I'm okay, but I have some if you'd rather I wear one."

"No." She pulled him down, and he went willingly. His hips settled between her legs, and he kissed her again. Her arms wrapped around his neck, and he rocked forward. Her body resisted his attempts at first, but he continued to move in and out. The heat and hot grip on his cock was an exquisite torture of the most unbelievable kind. He found a rhythm and moved his hips. He wouldn't last. God, she was so tight and felt so good.

Kayla constricted under him like a bow with the cord pulled tight. She gripped his biceps and ... fuck. She shattered as he watched. Her face bloomed in crimson, and her body gripped him in pulses. He lost any chance of holding off. Alex closed his eyes, lowered his head to her shoulder, and launched. His body moved out of primal instinct, his breathing stopped, and he saw explosions of color behind his closed eyes. As he stilled, he drew a shallow breath, then a deeper one, then he panted to fill his lungs.

Alex dropped beside Kayla and, with arms as weak as jelly, rolled her over so he could hold her. Her breath was just as desperate as his. He slid a hand up to the back of her neck and dropped a kiss on her forehead.

Kayla put a hand on his chest and patted him. He chuckled, and then so did she. "Why did we wait so long?" She punctuated the words with puffs of air.

"It wasn't long." He chuckled, although the week had seemed like a year.

Kayla jerked up onto her elbow. "That makes me easy, doesn't it?" Her eyes were wide and startled.

Alex moved up to his elbow. "No, it doesn't."

"Sure, it does. I only met you a couple of weeks ago or so. Now, I'm sleeping with you. I'm easy. Oh, crud." She lifted her thumbnail to her mouth and nipped at it.

He took her hand in his. "Easy is falling into bed with a man you just met."

"I just met you," she said, her face a portrait of worry.

"No, we've met, dated, talked, kissed, talked

more. You decided quickly, so did I, but neither of us is promiscuous nor easy." He moved to kiss her, and she pulled away.

"Are you sure?"

"Positive. Besides, who's going to know how soon we got physical? I'm not going to say anything to anyone. Are you?" He pushed her hair away from her face.

"No." She shook her head. "This feels so right."

He nodded. "It does. This is the best sex I've had."

She rolled her eyes. "You're just saying that."

Alex waited until she looked at him. "I don't lie, Kayla. I don't exaggerate. I can't remember a time I've felt this way. You and I, together, is magical."

She stared at him, and that smile ticked at the side of her mouth. "It was special, wasn't it?"

"Very," he agreed and rolled her onto her back. He would show her just how special it was at least two or three more times that night.

* * *

Alex pulled the crossover into a parking spot at Nail's shop. Nail had texted him at about six that morning and asked if he were dead in a snowbank somewhere. Alex replied with a middle finger emoji. He walked around and opened the door for Kayla, and taking her hand, they walked into the shop. "Oh, wow. This is nice." The showroom held a variety of classic and commissioned bikes.

"Nail and his dad do the best restorations and builds in the state." Alex dropped his arm over her shoulders.

"In the Tri-State area, actually." Nail came out of the back, wiping his hands. "Bull, glad you could come down and spend some time."

"Bull?" Kayla looked up at him.

"Short for Bullseye. He could shoot the center out of a target like no one else. I'm Brian, also called Nail, and no, we don't know why I got that name." He extended his hand.

Kayla shook his hand and laughed at him. Alex snorted. "We do know why, but we won't say in mixed company."

Nail barked out a laugh. "Yeah, that's okay with me."

"I like these. They're beautiful. Were the ones you saw like these?" Kayla asked Alex.

"That's why I was so upset." Alex glanced at Nail. "On two separate occasions, I saw custom bikes being transported in the bed of trucks, lying on their sides covered in plastic."

"What?" Nail whipped around. "Can you describe the bikes?"

"Sure." Alex gave him an account of both bikes.

"Shit. I'd bet my last dollar those were two of the bikes stolen from dealerships around the Hills."

"What?" Alex and Kayla spoke at the same time.

"Bull, I'll get Dickie from the Spearfish dealership on the phone. I want you to describe the bikes to him. His place was broken into, and three of his custom models were stolen. There was a break-in at a shop in Hot Springs. Two others were stolen, and all the parts the guy had were gone. They wiped him out." Nail trotted toward the back of the building.

Alex turned to Kayla. "You don't have to stay for this, and we'll be working on bikes after the dust settles."

"Okay." She nodded her head. "I'm bringing back lunch for all of us, though." She lifted onto her toes and kissed him. "I need to keep your stamina up." She winked at him and slipped out of his arms. He watched her get into the SUV and back up.

"Dude, you coming?" Nail called from the back of the building.

"On my way." Alex watched her pull out into traffic and turned to make his way back to the office.

CHAPTER 17

Kayla spent the morning going from store to store, looking for bargains. She had a plan routed out for the afternoon. But she stopped back into the motorcycle shop about noon with a bucket of chicken, all the fixings, and the soda Alex liked. Alex greeted her with a kiss that stole her breath, and then he showed her the rest of the shop before they ate.

They stopped in one room that had three tables covered in motorcycles or parts of motorcycles. Alex stopped at the last table. "This is the bike I'm going to buy."

She glanced at the frame and engine. There was just the engine and metal frame. A bunch of wires threaded through the holes in the metal tubing.

There wasn't even a seat on the motorcycle. "Ah, it looks ... not done."

He laughed and took her into the next room. "These are the painted parts and both seats."

"Oh, wow. That's really cool. Both seats? You could take me for a ride?"

He smiled and dropped for a kiss. "I thought I had last night, but yes, any time you want."

She felt her face flush. Trying to hide it, she glanced back at the painted parts. The black paint had a red fleck in it, and there was a badge of some sort on both sides of the tank. "What is that?"

"The unit badge for the 1SFOD-D. Our old unit. When I told him I wanted to buy it, he hand-painted it on both sides."

"Wow, he's talented."

"That he is," Alex agreed. He took her hand and showed her the paint booth and then the store-room-slash-parts section with rows and rows of boxes. She did a double-take at the office furniture.

"I know, right? They spend a fortune on everything but office furniture."

She leaned to the right and mimicked the slant of the chair behind the beat-up desk. "How could you sit in that and not fall out?"

"It takes talent," Brian said as he headed down

the hall. "I locked the front door. Let's eat some of that chow you brought." He rubbed his hands together and walked past them to the break room, where the coffeepot and a table with folding chairs were located.

She nibbled on a leg as the guys destroyed the rest of the bucket. She had no idea how they weren't a thousand pounds. "Did you see stolen motorcycles?"

Alex nodded but waited until he'd finished chewing before answering. "They stole the purple one from Sturgis. The one we saw when we were in the tow truck was like one that was stolen from a place in Nebraska."

She frowned. "Why are they taking them north?"

"From what the detective who was here said, they think it's a ring of thieves. While we only saw two, they thought most of the bikes were being sent to big cities to be repainted or fenced." Brian answered her question.

"But these guys had to know they were stolen. They had them laying down in the back of their trucks." Kayla took a bite of her chicken.

"That's what we figured. The detective was

going to alert the police up in Hollister, which means …"

"Ken," everyone said at the same time.

"He said something about the highway patrol being around at times, too," Kayla added, remembering their morning visit the first time she'd had breakfast with Alex.

"Dad said the guy was a dinosaur and needed to retire." Brian shook his head. "They need someone up there who can back up Ken."

"Ken said a new trooper was coming out from the center of the state. I didn't get the guy's name," Alex noted.

"Most of the people up there police themselves, that's for sure, but it's the people who travel through that bring the drama." Brian grabbed another piece of chicken. "Like the serial killer."

Kayla choked on a swallow of her Coke, and Alex reached over and patted her back. She coughed until she could breathe again. "What?" She squeaked the word.

"What, you guys don't know? That's the first story I heard up there. But then again, it was a few years back, so maybe they've moved on from that one."

"Dude, do I need to punch you? Fill us in." Alex gave his friend a look that Kayla would have taken as anger, but they both broke up laughing, and Brian told them the story as they finished their meal.

* * *

KAYLA STRETCHED LEISURELY, and as the pleasant ache of her body reminded her of Saturday night's marathon sex, she inhaled the most amazing scent. Sandalwood, musk, and a mixture of something so uniquely Alex that she couldn't help but inhale deeper. She rolled over on her side and moved closer to him.

"Good morning," he mumbled with his eyes still shut.

"Good morning," she replied, settling against him. "Do you need to go help Brian this morning?"

"Hmmm … for a little bit. We'll leave at noon, grab a bite, and head north." Alex didn't open his eyes. He looked so peaceful.

Kayla slid her finger down his muscled arm, tracing his biceps to his corded forearms. He was stunning to look at and so good to her in bed. He never finished first, always tending to her needs before he climaxed. Most of the lovers she'd had just rammed forward until they were done, with no effort to stimulate her other than what their cock was doing. Alex wasn't like that. He treated her like she was something special. A seed of sadness blossomed deep inside. No, she wouldn't mourn losing him before either of them actually left Hollister. She wouldn't let the future shadow the present and siphon her joy from today. She walked her fingers back up his arm. "I'll go buy all the things I scoped out yesterday."

He opened one eye. "Do you need any help?"

She laughed. "Shopping? No, I have that down to a science."

He wrapped his arm around her and sighed. "I'd like this weekend to go on forever."

"So would I." She trailed her fingers down his back. Touching him was irresistible.

He said something and then stopped.

"What?" She chuckled when he mumbled something she couldn't understand.

He drew a breath and then repeated louder, "I want you to spend time with me at the cabin when we're back at Hollister, but with the gossips in town, your reputation would be shot in less than twenty-four hours."

"My reputation? Good God, do people still talk

that way?" She pushed him onto his back and laid across his chest to see him. "Seriously?"

"I hear a lot of things when I'm at the diner. The problems people have had in the past and judgments that have been passed." He pushed her hair from her face. "I don't want you to be thought of as less because you're with me."

"Less? Because of you?" She didn't understand the logic. "Why would someone think that? Alex, I'm a big girl. I'm almost thirty. I don't need anyone's approval to be with someone I like."

"Even if people talk?"

Kayla snorted. "Let them talk." She loved people and generally thought the best of them, but if someone was going to snipe at her because she was attracted to Alex, let them.

"What about your uncle Phil?" He stared at her with those dark brown eyes.

"No, I don't want to spend the night with him."

Alex jerked and then barked out a laugh. "That's not what I meant."

"I know." She smiled at him. "He's my uncle. Sure, I'm going to let him and Aunt Sarah know, so they don't worry if I'm not back at a certain time, but I'm not going to ask permission. And if they don't like it, well, then..." She sighed.

A HOME FOR LOVE

"You can stay with me." Alex shrugged.

She rolled her eyes. "I'm not moving in with you. That would be way too quick. I was going to say we'll cross that bridge when we get to it."

Alex dipped his head and made a face. "Yeah, kind of fast for that step."

"It could be hard to explain to the girls."

"I think by the age of fourteen, Kimber would have a pretty good idea what you being gone all night means."

"True." She'd talk to Sarah before she talked to Phil. It did matter to her what her family thought, and she didn't want to cause problems.

"We could be inventive. You could come back to the cabin for lunch." She waggled her eyebrows at him.

"Quickies are not overrated." He laughed and rolled her, so he was on top of her. He glanced at the clock. "Shit. Is that the time?"

Kayla lifted her head and twisted to see the clock. "Wow. We really slept in."

"I've got to get over to the shop."

"We could shower together. It would save time." Kayla almost hid the laughter in her voice.

"I have a feeling it wouldn't. Go ahead. I'll text

Nail and let him know I'll be about a half hour late."

Kayla stood up and glanced over her shoulder. "Are you *sure* you couldn't be an hour late?"

Alex looked up from the bed. "He'll get over it." He dropped the phone and followed her into the bathroom.

* * *

KAYLA SPENT MORE money than she'd expected, but the sales were too good to resist. She'd filled the back of her crossover with bags, boxes, gifts, and a special gift for Alex. She'd purchased him an e-reader and a gift card so he could buy the books that intrigued him. For Uncle Phil, she found the perfect present. She got him a beer-making kit. He could craft his own beers and use different recipes. Granted, he liked to go to the bar for his beer, but he could have one on Saturday and Sunday now if he liked. One that he made.

After making sure Alex's gift was hidden, she grabbed the two dozen tacos and soda she'd bought for lunch. Kayla jiggled the bags to lock her crossover and headed inside the motorcycle showroom. The door made a loud buzzing sound as she opened it.

"In the back!" She heard Alex's voice and walked into the back, peering into each specialized room, looking for the two men. She found them in the room where Brian was building Alex's motorcycle. They had the gas tank on and handlebars installed.

"How did you know it was me ... Wow. Now, it looks like a motorcycle."

"We didn't, but we couldn't leave. It's shaping up," Brian said as he turned a wrench, tightening something. "Just one more."

"I've got it, no worries," Alex replied and glanced over at her. "Did you get everything done?"

"Yep. Oh, don't forget we need to stop to pick up Edna's pictures."

Brian snorted. "Do people still use film? I thought it was all digital these days."

Kayla shifted the food and drinks. "According to Edna, she's a purist. I'm going to put the food in the break room."

"We'll be there in a minute," Alex said.

Kayla put the food down and heard the loud bell from the front of the store. "Kayla, could you tell them I'll be right there?" Brian yelled from the other room.

"Sure." She marched out to the showroom. "Hi, welcome. Brian, the owner, will be out in a second. I think they're at a critical point in putting something together."

Two men turned from the bike they were looking at. "Are these customs?"

Kayla shoved her hands in her parka pockets. "Sir, I have no idea. They are pretty, though, aren't they?"

The other gentleman moved to a motorcycle displayed by the window. The guy who asked gave her a look that made her feel less than adequate and didn't respond. He bent down and looked at the motor. Well, that was rude, and she didn't like those guys. Something in the pit of her gut told her they weren't good people, and she generally liked everyone. When she got those vibes, it was unusual. Unusual enough for her to want one or both of the guys up front. Now.

"Alex, Brian," she called over her shoulder.

She heard tools hit the floor, and Alex led the way down the hall. Concern marred his expression. Brian looked curious but not upset.

A HOME FOR LOVE

"Everything okay?" Alex asked her. He put his hands on his hips and stared at the two customers.

"Are these custom builds or kits with modifications?" the same man asked without turning around to look at either Alex or Brian.

"All custom." Brian wiped his hands on a red shop rag. "Are you interested in buying? Someone already bought those."

"Do you build them?"

Brian nodded. "Under contract only. I don't do speculations."

"When are the owners coming for these?"

Alex moved in front of her and crossed his arms. "Why?"

"Just curious if I could make you an offer you don't want to refuse." The guy stood up and finally looked at them. He did a double-take. Kayla gave the guy a mental sneer. *That's right. These guys are huge.*

Brian snorted. "They're paid for. I'm not selling a contracted custom build to someone off the street, no offense. Not good business, especially since those three are sold to MC riders."

The guy huffed out a sound of disagreement. "Your loss." He walked out the door, and the other man followed him.

"I'm sorry to call you away from your work, but they gave me the creeps."

"Meh, we get all types in here. The MC guys who commissioned those bikes look like they don't have two dollars to rub together, and they could probably buy and sell this shop twice over. Those two just now weren't here to buy. They just wanted to act like they were something."

Alex dropped his arm over Kayla's shoulder. "Lunch, and then we need to head north."

"Did you catch up on all your work?" She looked back at Brian as they walked down the hall to the break room.

"We did. This guy is good at what he does." Brian clasped Alex on the shoulder.

"More like I take care of the simple stuff so you can do the more complex issues. But I'm happy to help. Do you need me to come down next week?" Alex pulled out a chair for Kayla and helped her take off her coat, draping it over the back.

"No, man, I thought I told you. The old man got clearance to start back in the shop on light duty next week. We had a long talk, and he'll be doing the paperwork in the morning and tinkering on the customs in the afternoon if he feels up to it. I think I've finally convinced him if he wants to make a full recovery, slow and steady sets the pace."

Kayla took a taco out of the pack and grabbed a packet of hot sauce. "Brian, do you have plans for the middle of December?"

"Just work. Why?" Brian spoke around the food in his mouth. "Sorry."

"That's okay. Hollister is doing a decoration thing. The whole town is going to be there for it. Maybe you and your dad could come up. I know Uncle Phil talks highly of Tank."

"Phil really made Dad feel at home up there when I was talking with Dr. Wheeler. I'll see what he wants to do. Knowing the old man, he'll want to have the doors open. We're going to have to push hard to finish the bikes that are Christmas presents." He held up a hand when Alex whipped his head up to speak. "We can do it, and if we get behind, I'll call. You helping me clear the maintenance work was enough to get us back on schedule."

Alex pointed at Brian. "Make damn sure you do call. I can be here any weekend."

Kayla smiled when Brian rolled his eyes. "Yes, Mother."

"Watch it. You already owe me roses and

chocolates."

"For what?" Kayla didn't hesitate to ask the question.

"He thought you were like sixteen."

She blinked. "What?"

"So not fair. He said Phil's niece. Phil's daughters are that age, so naturally, I assumed you were—"

"Wow, *way* too young," Kayla finished for him.

"Exactly." Alex grabbed another taco out of the box. "Like I'd ever."

"I apologized, man."

"Not well enough. I don't see the roses and chocolate."

"Make him get you *See's* chocolates from one of the shops in California where they hand make them. They're the absolute best. My mom and I got them shipped in from California. Only for special occasions like birthdays and such. So good."

Alex pointed to her but looked at Brian. "There you go. That's what I want."

Brian leaned forward to stare at her. "You're no help. Thank you."

She pointed to Alex. "You thought *he* was dating a *teenager*. You're welcome."

Brian stared at her, and then his face split into a smile. He turned to Alex. "I like her."

Alex frowned and leaned forward so she couldn't see Brian, then growled, "Get your own woman."

Brian laughed, bent backward, and winked at her. The friendship between the two was amazing to watch.

CHAPTER 18

Alex grabbed the waste oil from the oil change he'd just completed. He hefted the bucket, heading to the drum that the recycling people would come for when it was full. "Phil, we've got about two more oil changes before the drum will be full." He carefully poured the oil into the collection barrel.

"I'll let them know." The response came from closer than Alex thought it would. He turned to see Phil almost beside him.

"Kayla talked to her aunt and me."

Alex gave Phil a quick glance. "Okay …"

"She says you and her are together."

Alex drew a deep breath and stopped pouring the oil to concentrate on the conversation. Well, that was quick. He'd had dinner with Kayla and her family last night when they'd come back from Rapid. He wasn't expecting that conversation until much later.

"Do you have a problem with that?" He'd had people he thought were friends pull up stakes before.

"No. No, I do not. She's a grown woman, and you're an adult. I just don't want to see her hurt."

Alex leaned against the drum he'd been filling. "I thought we'd had this conversation before."

"Just repeating what bears repeating." Phil looked down and toed the concrete floor. "You're a good man, Alex. Damn excellent mechanic, too. Don't want you two to get into a tussle, her to get hurt, or you to walk away. Wouldn't be good."

Alex hid the smile that twitched at the corners of his mouth. "Phil. I won't hurt her, nor will I leave one minute before you tell me you can handle this shop by yourself."

Phil cleared his throat and looked up at the roof. "That's just it. I've been hanging on by myself. You've seen the workload. I'm not complaining, mind you, but if there were two people working, things would be better around here."

Alex cocked his head. "Are you offering me a full-time position?"

Phil nodded. Once. "Would you be interested?"

Alex was dumbfounded. "Yes."

Phil nodded. "Gotta work on your pay."

"What's wrong with what you're paying me now?" He was making enough money with his medical retirement to live like a king in Hollister. Plus, he had money tucked away. Twenty-five percent of the profits from this shop was enough that he'd never worry about money.

Phil shook his head. "Not enough, but I don't know how much more we can do."

"How about this? After a year, we'll readdress the pay. Stay with it the way it is now and next year around Thanksgiving time, we'll put our heads together and see if it needs to be tweaked."

"You'd be willing to do that?" Phil asked.

"Absolutely. I'll need to find a permanent place to stay, though. I'm sure whoever gave me the cabin to use wasn't planning on me staying long term."

"I can talk to Mr. Marshall. We'll come to some arrangement, I'm sure." Phil extended his left hand. "Not a proper handshake, but it's all I can do right now. I'll get the paperwork drawn up, so it's legal, with the review of pay in a year included in it."

"Thank you. Oh, Phil, when you get out of the cast and can handle things, I'll need to get my stuff from storage and buy a truck." There was no mention of time off in the current contract.

"That won't be a problem. You really took a load of worry off my shoulders, son. A load of worry. I was afraid I would lose the business I have because I couldn't get to it fast enough. These ranchers and farmers need the equipment and would cart it down south if they thought it would take too long for me to get to it. It was getting to that point before I fell and broke my elbow." Phil smiled from ear to ear. "Maybe Sarah was right. She said everything happens for a reason. Maybe you were meant to be right here in this place. Maybe I needed to be sat on my ass so I could take a hard look at the work I had and what I can and can't do."

"It could be," Alex agreed. Looking back, it did feel like the universe had converged and pointed him directly to Hollister. Maybe it put Phil on his ass at the same time.

"Finish with that oil and then go grab your lunch before you get behind on your schedule."

Phil turned to leave but stopped and faced him again. "Alex, you take good care of my niece, and if anyone mutters a sideways word, you let me know. I know where the skeletons are buried in this town. No one will say anything about my niece staying with you occasionally. Consenting adults don't need anyone in their business." Phil lifted his chin and strutted to the front of the garage.

Alex chuckled and picked up the bucket of used oil. The thought of staying in Hollister had been niggling at him since Kayla had talked about her store. His nest egg wasn't big enough to buy the bike from Nail, even at a reduced rate, and to build a house. It would make a good down payment on the construction, though. He ran through options for a permanent place to stay as he cleaned up.

He waved at Phil, who was pumping gas, on his way to the diner. Kayla pulled up just as he hit the boardwalk. "Hey, you. What are you doing here?" He bent down and kissed her.

"I talked to Uncle Phil and Aunt Sarah last night. Then I slept in, and I didn't get to town before you went to work, and Uncle Phil was right behind me. I didn't want you to be blindsided. You didn't answer your phone."

Alex put his arm around her. "I normally put

my phone in my coat at work. Answering it when I'm under a rig isn't exactly easy. And you said *all* that with one breath." Alex laughed and pulled out his phone. "Look, I have a call from you."

Kayla blinked up at him. "He talked to you already, didn't he?"

"Oh, yeah." Alex nodded.

Kayla deflated. "I'm sorry."

"I'm not. Come have lunch with me, and I'll fill you in."

She turned with him to go to the diner. "On what?"

"The full-time position your uncle offered me."

Kayla spun around. "Really?"

"Yep." Alex nodded.

She squealed, threw her arms around his neck, and toed up to kiss him. Alex broke the kiss off when the door to the diner opened. Ken Zorn walked out, putting on his cowboy hat. "Hey, Alex. I got a call about those motorcycles you saw. Can we talk about that for a moment?"

"Sure. We were just heading in for lunch. Care to join us?"

Ken narrowed his eyes at Alex. "The last time I joined Kayla for a meal, you were throwing daggers at me from across the table." He crossed his arms over his chest.

"Were you?" Kayla glanced from Ken to him.

"Probably," Alex admitted. "But I think I'll be able to refrain. Now." He winked at Kayla, and her face turned a brilliant shade of red.

Ken chuckled. "Then after you."

"Hey, Ken, decide to eat after all?" Corrie, the server who worked afternoons, asked as Ken came back in.

"I'll eat with Alex and Kayla." He nodded.

Corrie smiled. "Three specials coming up. Two soda pops for gents, and what can I get for you, Kayla?"

"Water, please," she said as Alex helped her out of her coat. Finding their seats, they saw Edna nearby. "Oh, hi, Edna. I have your pictures." Kayla reached back into her coat and pulled out a packet of photographs.

"Thank you." Edna smiled at her. "How was the shopping in Rapid?"

Kayla strayed toward the table. "I got everything I needed and then some." Alex waited patiently for Kayla as she spoke with the women. Kayla laughed when the ladies at Edna's table laughed. "Are you ready for Thursday night?"

"We are," Doris Altham said. "Bernice and I are going to work on her quilt first. We've helped Edna pull all of Paul's shirts out of storage."

"Yep, I washed them all up. I think I'll have enough material to make a quilt with nothing but his shirts."

"Well, if not, we can extend the border and make it work." Kayla tapped the photograph packet. "Enjoy your pictures." Moving out of Corrie's way when Corrie delivered their food, she bumped into Alex.

She looked up at him. "Sorry."

"Don't be." He let her scoot into the booth and then sat down beside her.

Ken leaned forward, having already sat. "The briefing I got was the law enforcement people down south believe there's a ring of thieves targeting high-end motorcycle shops." He smiled and waited for Corrie to finish delivering their sodas and Kayla's water. "But they also think it could be bigger. Some custom car shops have been broken into in the tri-state area. They're forming a multi-state inquiry to see if the MO is the same. Can you tell me what drew your attention to the vehicles and what you saw?"

"Sure." Alex put his arm around Kayla. "I went

to get Kayla in Phil's big rig when her vehicle had a flat tire and shorted out. On the way back into town, we followed a POS pickup. I couldn't see the plates because they were caked in ice and grime from the road. But in the back, on its side, was an old, I'm talking really expensive kind of old, Shovelhead. It looked like it was in pristine condition. The plastic tarp was caught under it, and it was flapping in the wind. If you can afford something like that, you don't lay it down in the bed of a truck."

"Okay." Ken jotted something down in a pocket notebook he had on the table. "What about the other one?"

"We were here for breakfast on Friday morning. This guy comes in and asks if we know who ran the pumps. He was damn near out of gas. I filled him up. As I was pumping, a gust of wind blew the corner of the tarp up, and I saw brand-new tread. I lifted it, and it was a custom bike. Really noticeable. Purple paint with vanishing flames. Beautiful. I asked where he got the bike, and the guy overreacted. Shoved a fifty at me and told me to mind my own business. When we went down to Rapid, I talked with my friend, Brian. I believe you know him." Alex paused, and Ken nodded.

"Tank's son. I've met him a couple of times."

"Alex mentioned it when we were talking with him, and he told us about the thefts in the areas," Kayla added as Corrie placed plates of lasagna, French bread, and side salads on the table. She also placed three dressings in the center of the table.

"Anything else I can get you?"

"No, this is more than enough." Kayla laughed.

"Oh, girl, that comes with dessert." She winked at Kayla. "Chocolate pie. Save room."

Kayla looked at Alex. "That's all on you. I'll be lucky to eat a quarter of this."

Alex chuckled. "We should have split the meal."

"Yes, we should have," she agreed, puffing up her cheeks like a chipmunk.

Ken took a bite of his food and then asked, "Was there anything similar between the two incidents?"

Alex thought for a moment. "Both trucks were older. The first one was a wreck, but it was moving at a good clip, especially for the road conditions. Both bikes were on their side." He shook his head. "That's a crime, right there."

"The guy had a sharp accent. He wasn't from

around here," Kayla said before she took a bite of bread.

"What makes you say that?" Ken asked.

She shrugged and finished the food in her mouth before she answered. "Well, he talked different. I had a professor in college who talked like that. He was from New Hampshire. Just a different way of saying things, that's all."

"Can you describe him to me?"

Alex nodded. "Six feet, probably one-eighty. Dark brown hair, at least a two-day's growth of beard. Wore black jeans, boots, and dark blue winter coat."

Ken jotted that down and asked, "Did you get a glimpse of the guy driving the truck you first saw?"

"No. Did you?" he asked Kayla.

"Nope. I was still an ice cube." She exaggerated a shiver beside him.

"I'll keep an eye open for trucks hauling loads with tarps while on patrol. If you see anything like that again, try to get a license plate and call me. You have my number, right?"

Both Kayla and he shook their heads. Ken blinked in surprise. "Well, that's a first." He pulled out a business card. "That's my cell phone. If you go through dispatch, it just delays my response.

A HOME FOR LOVE

Out here, it can take long enough for me to get to where I need to be. I'll call it in on the way to whatever you need me to respond to."

Alex nodded. "Does that highway patrol officer ever help?"

"Sure, sure." Ken nodded. "But he's now officially using his last vacation days before he retires, so it's just me for the time being. The troopers have someone moving out here to take his territory, but who knows when that will be? I'm assuming some of the others will cycle through to keep a presence in the area."

"Oh my God!" Edna shrieked behind him. Alex jumped up, and his leg screamed at the jarring twist. Ken was right beside him.

"What's wrong?" Kayla twisted around in the booth to look at Edna.

The woman's hand shook as she held a photograph out toward Ken. "It can't be."

"What?" everyone in the diner said at the same time.

"Is that … Bigfoot?" Edna handed the photograph to Ken. Ken made a face and then looked at it. His eyes popped open, and he looked again.

The diner was so noisy because everyone was talking at once. Alex leaned over and studied the picture. He leaned down. The photo was good, but the image she was referencing was in the background. He'd seen that silhouette before. That *wasn't* Bigfoot. It was a man wearing a ghillie suit. He leaned over and whispered the same to Ken.

Ken pursed his lips. "Don't tell anyone else that. I'll explain later." He then handed the photo back to Edna. The crowd seemed to stop talking immediately. All eyes were on Ken. He shrugged. "I can't tell for sure, but it could be, Edna. Could very well be."

The woman grabbed the photo, and everyone, including Kayla, leaned over to see what was on the photograph.

"Why did you …" Alex frowned when Ken nodded for them to move to the corner of the room. Alex followed him over. No one in the diner noticed. They were all huddled over the picture and talking at once.

"Did you see the date in the corner?"

"No." Alex was looking at the man in the ghillie suit. "Look, I saw that silhouette through a scope enough times to know what that is."

"I know." Ken rubbed his face. "You're going to have to trust me on this. I need to go out to the Marshall ranch. Now." He reached for his wallet.

"I got this." Alex waved at the table.

"Thanks. I'll explain when I can or get someone to come talk to you. I got to go, but I need something first." Ken moved back to Edna. "May I take a picture of your picture?"

Edna glanced up at Ken. "You think this could be a real Bigfoot sighting?"

"Edna, I don't know, but I'd like to have a photo of this in case I need it."

"Oh, sure, sure. Should I tell the media? The television people? Or should I post it on social media? This is a gigantic find!"

"No," Ken said firmly. "If this is Bigfoot, we'd have all those people hunting it up here. You don't want to be responsible for someone coming in and killing or capturing it, do you?"

Edna's face dropped, and she shook her head. "He's caused no issues with us. But this is an amazing picture. Isn't it?"

"I tell you, Edna, that's a one-in-a-million photo. I'd keep it safe somewhere. When I get back, we can talk about what you should and shouldn't do with that photo. The responsible thing for the community, for our children," Ken said and then took a picture of the picture with his phone.

Edna nodded. Suddenly serious. "The town needs to be protected, and as I said, if anyone has seen him before, no one has said. There has been no theft or anything, has there? Mauled animals?" She looked up at Ken.

"No, ma'am. This guy seems to keep to himself. I've had no one say anything about seeing a Bigfoot." Alex would bet that was the God's honest truth.

That set the diner into another frenzy of conversation. Ken glanced at Alex as he turned. "I'll keep you in the loop on everything."

Alex sat back down and watched as Ken got into his patrol vehicle and hightailed it out of town.

"That is exciting, even if it turns out to be nothing." Kayla chuckled and stabbed some lettuce with her fork. "Bigfoot and a permanent job in Hollister all in one day. Doesn't get more exciting than that."

Alex agreed and took a bite of his lasagna. *Only it did get more exciting, especially if men in ghillie suits were in the area, but it was pretty damn obvious Ken didn't want that mentioned.* He listened to the boisterous conversation as he finished his food. Kayla barely touched hers. Instead, she turned in the booth and visited with the rest of the people who'd forgotten they'd paid for lunch. Alex didn't know why Ken didn't tell Edna, but he knew enough to keep his mouth shut. Sooner or later, he'd find out what had sent Ken out of there like his tail was on fire.

CHAPTER 19

Alex was ass-up and head down in a diesel motor when he heard the door open and close. He recognized Phil's voice but not the other. It didn't matter. Phil took care of the customer service aspect of the business. Alex turned the wrenches, and that was perfect for him.

"Yo, newb."

Alex rolled his eyes and straightened. "You know I medically retired as a Sergeant First Class. That newb shit needs to go."

Billy sniggered. "About time you told me off." He leaned against a tractor tire. "Got a second? Need to give you a sitrep."

Alex put down his wrench and grabbed a rag to wipe off his hands. "Go for it."

Billy looked around and then back at him. "Ever hear of Guardian Security?"

"I have. They recruit the Force, or they did before their operation got blown to hell."

"I work for Guardian. We have an annex of sorts out at the Marshall ranch. The cabin you're staying in is a Guardian asset."

Alex leaned against the vehicle he was working on. "Did you come here to tell me you need it back?" That would suck. But he could manage now that the bitter cold snap had passed.

"Nah, man. I came here to tell you that guy in the ghillie suit was one fucker who attacked the ranch at the same time the DC location was blown to hell."

Alex blinked. "Fuck."

"Exactly. The ranch survived. Those fuckers didn't. That's why the deputy didn't say shit to you. Everyone here knows Guardian is at the ranch. No one will confirm it. It's the best-kept secret that everyone in the territory knows."

Alex crossed his arms. "Hollister is full of good people."

"And crazy ones who think UFOs and Bigfoot exist." Billy laughed. "She's harmless unless she goes public with the photo. Anyone with a good sight picture or magnification program could tell what that was and what it wasn't."

"So, what are you going to do?"

"Me? Nothing. Mr. Marshall, the guy who owns the ranch, will take care of it. I don't know how, but when the man says he'll do something, he'll do it."

Alex nodded. "What do you need from me?"

"Two things. First, your word that you'll keep this shit under wraps."

"That's a fucking no-brainer. We protect our own. Guardian is in the brotherhood. What's the second?"

"Do you have any interest in teaching?" Billy crossed his legs, leaning harder against the tractor wheel. "Figured you'd need something permanent."

"Phil just offered me a permanent gig, and I accepted, but I wouldn't be averse to helping occasionally. I totally fucked my leg, man, but I can do classroom or firing line instruction. Just can't move the way I need to actually do the job."

"The two instructors we have are still working in the field. I'm one. Isaac is the other one. You met him at the Spur. We don't have a full-time class load, but when we have to leave, it could cause a delay in classes. If you could teach at night, or maybe an afternoon and the weekends, we could keep them moving and out into the field. You'd be called to fill in occasionally after we get you up to speed."

"I could do that. I'd check with Phil first, but as long as I keep my stuff tight here, I should be able to manage it. I got to tell you, not knowing in advance when I'd be called out sucks, though."

Billy nodded. "I get it. We'd give you as much notice as possible, and if you can't do it, then you can't."

Alex frowned and looked down at his worn boots. He wanted to help. To teach would be different, but he could wrap his head around it. "I'll teach. I'd be available some evenings and some weekend days to get up to speed, but I have commitments here."

"Commitments?" Billy frowned.

"A new relationship. I'm not going to let that suffer to do this." Kayla had become important to him in a brief time. Opportunities be damned, nothing was more important than figuring out where his feelings about the crazy, intriguing, impossibly energetic, sexy woman were going to go. They were burning hot, and he wanted to keep the fires stoked.

"Ah, well, that I can understand. You wouldn't be able to tell anyone what you're doing out there. The cover would be you're working on equipment."

"Makes sense." He nodded. "Phil?"

"You can tell him you're helping Guardian. That's all he needs to know. Believe me, he won't ask. Guardian has helped that man. He's loyal."

Alex nodded. There was obviously a lot about that little town he didn't know. "That works."

Billy lifted away from the tractor. "About the cabin."

Damn, he figured it would be needed sooner or later. "When do you need me out?"

The man snorted. "Nah, it comes with the gig. Yours until you don't need it. No rent. Guardian will send you the contract and pay details."

"I'll give you my email address."

"Dude, they already have it. They know everything there is to know about you, or they wouldn't have made the offer." Billy gave him a two-finger salute and moseyed out of the shop. Phil was up and out of the chair by the time the door closed.

Alex was staring at the ground, his arms still crossed and thinking about the turns and twists his life had taken. All because he said he'd come up to see Phil's shop. Damn. Blessing was more than woo-woo. She was a guiding light, wasn't she?

"Everything okay?"

Alex blinked, startled out of his thoughts. "Yes, I'll be working part-time at the Marshall ranch. Only when needed. You know, when equipment breaks, and they need someone to step in."

Phil scratched his cheek with his left hand. "Still working here, though?"

"Not going to interfere with this job. I won't let it. I'm also good with the cabin. Part of the deal."

Phil visibly relaxed. "Good. That's good. Hey, did you hear Edna thinks she has a picture of Bigfoot?" Phil cackled a laugh. "That woman is insane."

Alex chuckled. "I heard that."

"You need any help with this one?" Phil pointed to the semi he was working on.

"Nah, I'm just finishing up. Give me an hour or so to put her back together. It was a simple fix. Just had to take apart damn near the whole engine to get to it." He looked up at the late-model semi. "She'll be good for years to come. Most of these ranchers take damn good care of their equipment."

"They do. I'll let the Marshalls know they can pick her up in the morning, then." Phil used a pencil to scratch his arm. "Now, we just need to find a shop for Kayla."

Alex's jaw dropped open. "How in the hell did you know about that?"

"I know that girl." Phil lifted his chin. "And Gen told me she was asking about storefront property. I figured she won't take help from me."

"She wants to do it on her own," Alex agreed. "She didn't want you to know in case she can't find anything."

"Well ..." Phil glanced around like someone would magically appear from behind a tractor or truck in the shop. "You make sure she comes to the Decoration Day this Saturday. She needs to be there."

Alex narrowed his eyes. "Why? What did you do?"

"Just made a casual comment to someone who might help. If it happens, it happens. If it doesn't, well, then it doesn't." The older man groaned and jabbed the pencil in his cast farther.

"You're going to lose that thing up there," Alex said. "Go online and buy a can of cast spray."

"What?"

"You spray it in your cast, and it stops the itch."

Alex motioned to Phil's arm. "Didn't anyone tell you that was a thing?"

"Hell, no." Phil spun. "I'll even pay for expedited shipping."

Alex shook his head. God, he loved this town.

CHAPTER 20

Kayla stood in front of the mirror.

"Wow. You look great," Kimber said from her doorway.

"Do you think so? It isn't too … shiny?" The shimmer of the black material caught in the room's overhead light and glimmered across the surface of the silky material.

"No, it's beautiful. I like this part." Kimber touched the drooping cowl neck on the front and back of the dress. Kayla had changed the pattern to make it more modest. The cowl in the pattern went to the small of the back, but she'd adapted the pattern to show a portion of her back between her shoulder blades. The front cowl hinted at a glimpse of cleavage. The dress was formfitting but not too tight. It fell to her knees. The strappy shoes she wore were actually her mother's.

"Thank you. I'm so excited about today." She'd finished the pattern part of her quilt and was on track to finish the present by Christmas. "I wish I could go to the dance." The girl sat down on Kayla's bed. "Dad says it's for adults."

"Well, there'll be alcohol, and I don't believe anyone is bringing children. Besides, you and Carol are making money babysitting tonight."

"Jared and Scott are great kids. Cody will just watch television, so it won't be hard." Kimber smiled. "Can you help me make a dress for our spring dance at school?"

"A spring dance? Oh, I have a thousand ideas." Kayla sat down beside her cousin. "Do you want me to teach you how to make clothes?"

"Can you do that?"

"Oh, sure. It isn't too difficult."

"Mom says it is." Kimber tried not to laugh.

"No one showed your mom how to do it properly." Kayla rolled her eyes. "And besides, she can crochet like a dream, so don't discount her skill."

"Never. She's the best," Kimber agreed. "Are you going to help in town with the Christmas decorations?"

"I am. I'm going to hang this up and get changed. Are you and Carol going to help?"

"The school had a sign-up sheet. We're manning the hot cocoa station. Of course, we're making Momma's recipe. That's how we got the prime spot."

"Where's it at?" Kayla asked as she slipped out of her dress.

"Out front of Gen's diner. But Dad is running extension cords for a space heater." Kimber laughed. "Tessa is so jealous. She's at the community hall cleaning up."

"Who's Tessa?"

"The girl who likes the same boy that I do." Kimber shrugged. "He's helping with putting the lights on the tree."

"Ah, gotcha." Kayla chuckled. "Well, I'll be by a couple of times for sure. Alex and I have no idea what we're doing. We're just showing up."

"That's what most of the town is doing. That's why Miss Prentiss said we should know what we're doing before we get there because there'll be enough confusion already."

Kayla tugged a bulky sweater over her head. "Sounds like Miss Prentiss should be in charge of everything today."

"She'd be the best at it. She's a great teacher," Kimber agreed. "Can I get a ride into town with you? Dad's already gone, and Mom won't go in until closer to noon. She's cooking a bunch of chili. Gen is making the cornbread, and I think others are bringing chili, too."

"Happy to give you a lift. What about Carol?" Kayla slid her foot into her tennis shoes. She had snow boots to change into when it came time to work.

"She went with Dad. She likes to help him at the shop. I'm not much into greasy stuff."

Kayla fought back a reply. She wasn't into that either, but men who worked with greasy stuff, oh, yes, ma'am, she was very much into them—or him, actually.

"Okay, I'm ready. Are you?"

"You bet."

* * *

Kayla ducked past a mountain of lights with legs and opened the door to the community hall. "Thank you," the person under the lights said.

"Anytime," she replied as they lumbered from the community hall to a truck in the parking lot.

She went back inside and stood to the side of the door, staring at the chaos. There were people everywhere. Strings of light, candy canes, and a star with a dimming glow scattered across the floor. She heard Alex and moved to the right, past people who were lined up to help.

"We'll need this next batch taken over to the tree site."

"I can do that," a man said. Alex pointed to the batch of lights he was talking about. "Have the kids finished putting together the ornaments?" Alex asked someone behind him.

"Yes." The woman's reply came back.

"Can I get someone with a truck to take all the ornaments over to the tree site? The Marshalls will be here shortly with the tree, and they'll stake it out, but we'll need all the lights and ornaments over there when they arrive."

"I've got it," Phil said. "I'll need some help loading and unloading."

"I'll help," Kayla said from the back. "I can put what doesn't fit in Uncle Phil's truck in the back of my SUV."

"Good." Alex smiled at her. "Kathy, can we get a couple of the older kids to help load up the truck?"

"On it," the same woman's voice said from one of the side rooms.

Alex said something to Jeremiah Wheeler and then headed her way, letting Dr. Wheeler take over the direction. "All right, we need the power pole decorations to head into town next. Ladies, these are light and can fit in a car. Who can help?"

Alex weaved through people until he reached her. He bent down and gave her a chaste kiss. "Good morning." He glanced up and then backed her out of the building. Outside, he grabbed her and pulled her in for a kiss that, as always, stole her breath, her thoughts, and her heart.

When he lifted away from her, she sighed. "It is a good morning now."

"Much better." Alex smiled at her.

"You were quite the taskmaster in there."

Alex snorted. "Doc Wheeler had to leave and asked me to step in. I did. Then I stepped out." He pointed to one of the side doors. "Let's go get those decorations."

Kayla fell in step with Alex and the rest of the town. The Marshalls did, in fact, deliver a thirty-foot pine tree that was absolutely beautiful. Workers from the ranch staked it into the ground with massive pins and metal cables, which held it straight. The men used a bucket truck that Cane Phelps had gotten permission from the power company to use. They strung the high lights, affixed the star, and used the smaller ornaments to decorate the tree. Of course, the women were on the ground directing the placement of the bulbs. Kayla had never laughed so hard in her life.

"No, your other right. Quick Draw!" one lady said, causing the man in the bucket to pull the bulb in. He lowered the bucket, opened the door, and invited her in. She walked in, kissed him full on the lips, and they lifted back into the air.

"Who's that?" She laughed.

"That's Dixon Marshall and his wife Joy," Gen said from beside her. "Great people. They have a beautiful little girl."

"She didn't come to the quilting social."

"No, she's more into other things, or so I hear."

"Other things?"

"Like martial arts. Someone was telling me she teaches it, too. I was thinking about asking her if she'd be willing to teach a self-defense class for all the women come summer. I mean, sure, the guys are always around ... until they aren't."

"That's not a bad idea." Kayla nodded.

"Oh, hey, Senior."

An older man came up and hugged Gen. "Morning. Where's Andrew?"

"Up on that ladder." Gen pointed to where he and Ciera's husband Scott were hanging a huge garland.

"Oh, Senior, this is Kayla Bryce, Phil Granger's niece. Senior is my father-in-law, Andrew Hollister, Senior. We call him Senior to keep things from getting confusing," Gen said.

"Oh, you're the quilting seamstress?" the older man asked. Kayla saw the twinkle in his eye.

"You're lucky I'm not a dancing, quilting seamstress. That could be dangerous." Kayla extended her hand. "It's a pleasure to meet you, sir."

"And you. You know, I was thinking this town could use a small clothing store." He glanced down the street. "The Sandersons were talking about building a bakery to expand their grocery store. I think that's a smart idea. Since I own most of this land, I told them I'd put up the building right there, past your uncle's garage. I can add to that building if you'd be interested."

Kayla stared up at the man. "What?"

The man frowned. "What part didn't you hear?"

"Why would you build me a store?"

Gen put her hand on Kayla's arm. "Kayla, most

of the people in town don't own the land or the buildings they're in. I own the diner, Phil owns the garage and the acreage behind it, and Declan owns some acreage that the Bit and Spur sits on. Everyone else has a lease with Senior for their business."

"Oh." Kayla's mind spun with ideas and competing thoughts. "Mr. Senior, I'd love to have a shop, but I'd like to talk to you about what I was thinking about as a business plan. I don't want to disappoint anyone."

Senior smiled. "It's just Senior. Young lady, would you care to join me for a cup of coffee at the diner? We can visit."

"I'd love to." Kayla took Senior's arm, and they strolled down to the diner.

"What do you think of Hollister?" Senior asked.

"Oh." She sighed and smiled. "This place is a mirage."

Senior cocked his head and looked down at her. "Care to explain that?"

"You know, when you see a mirage, and you keep driving, but you never get there?"

"I've heard of the concept, yes."

"Well, sir, I reached that beautiful place. I don't have to drive any farther." She smiled up at him.

"Other places have more money, job, industry, and such." Senior stopped and looked up and down the street.

"Sure, but I've been all over the world with my mom before she passed. I've seen those places. None of them have what this town has."

"And what's that?"

Kayla thought about it for a moment. "They're not home."

Senior smiled. "That's the truth, isn't it?" He patted her hand, and they stepped up onto the boardwalk of the diner. The weather was cold and crisp, but not uncomfortably so. "Cocoa?" Kimber asked as they approached.

"I'll be back out for some. I'm going to talk with Mr. Hollister first," Kayla promised.

"Why don't we take two and have cocoa instead of coffee?" Senior pulled out his wallet. "How much?"

"No, sir, we aren't charging. Mom and Dad donated the cocoa for Decoration Day," Kimber said and ladled two mugs full out of the crock pot. The steam rose in the air, and the smell of chocolate was wonderful.

"Well, thank you." Senior looked around. "Do you have marshmallows?"

Carol giggled. "Yes, sir. Would you like some?"

"My girl, cocoa isn't cocoa without marshmallows," Senior said seriously.

Carol handed him a hand-wrapped packet of marshmallows and then gave Kayla one. Kayla smiled and waved at her cousins as they went into the diner. Kayla waved at Edna, who was deep in conversation with an older man about the same age as Senior. Edna nodded to her. But Kayla could tell the woman was in a deep conversation.

"How about here?" Senior indicated a booth.

"Perfect."

"So, tell me your plans." The man opened his marshmallows and poured them on top of the hot cocoa. He pointed to her packet. "Need to get them melting. Cocoa is a serious business."

Kayla laughed and opened her packet, dumping the white clouds of sugar into her cocoa. "What I was envisioning was a small stock of new clothes. Jeans, socks, work shirts. Not a lot, and I'd only stock the common sizes unless someone requested something specific. Then, and this is still tentative, I thought of putting in a consignment area. Secondhand clothing, but only items that can be used again. I'd take a small percentage, but the consignee would get most of the money. With the way children grow, I thought it could be useful." She leaned forward. "And I'm a seamstress. I love making clothes, so I would take in orders, and I can alter, mend, etcetera. That would be the back of the shop. On one side, I'd like to make and sell quilts. I was thinking I could also do that online, but I'd make them to sell locally, too."

Senior nodded and took a sip of his cocoa. The melted marshmallow stuck to his lip. Kayla tried not to laugh, but when Senior swiped his tongue over his lip and still missed it, she cracked up. He grabbed a paper napkin and wiped his mouth, laughing, too. "I like your ideas. I'd like to offer a bit of a suggestion, if I may."

"Sure. Anything."

"You call around to the ranches and tell them you're setting up. Ask if there's anything they need to be stocked regularly. You'd be surprised. You can get the telephone numbers from the Sandersons. That's how they got a sense of what to stock in their grocery."

"That's an excellent idea." She watched as Edna got up and shook the gentleman's hand. He watched her leave and then headed their way.

"Senior," the man said, pulling out a piece of candy.

"Frank. This is Kayla Bryce. This is Frank Marshall. He owns the Rocking M. Big ranch south and east of here. Kayla's going to open up a clothing and sewing shop in the building that's going in at the end of the street."

"Next to the new bakery?" Frank popped the candy into his mouth.

"Yup," Senior said. "What's up with Edna?"

Frank Marshall shrugged. "Bit of business. You seen my missus?"

"Nope. Joy is up in the bucket telling Dixon what to do." Senior laughed.

Frank grunted. "Sounds about right. Talk with you later, Senior. Nice to meet you, Ms. Bryce."

Kayla smiled as the cowboy put on his coat and hat and headed down the street.

"He's good people if you don't mind that he talks in grunt."

Kayla turned to look at Senior. "What?"

"You'll figure it out. Now, we need to talk lease. Normally, what I do is give you a lifetime lease on the building. You need to make sure everything is clean, and if there's a problem you can't fix, you contact me. I'm a reasonable landlord, but I don't want to fix your dripping faucet."

Kayla nodded. "But you'll repair the heater if it goes out?"

"That I will."

"How much will it cost? I have some money set aside, and I should be able to pay for six months or so. Hopefully, the business will be established by then."

"I don't charge for the first year. No business in my town needs to worry about getting off the ground and paying rent. You pay for the utilities. After the first year, we'll sit down and discuss rent. You can talk to the other people around here. I'm fair. I don't need your money. I need Hollister to grow at a reasonable rate to support the people who choose to live here and on neighboring ranches."

"Sir, no offense, but that's almost too good to be true." Kayla couldn't help feeling like she was being set up. Nothing that good had ever fallen into her lap.

"Here's the thing. There *are* going to be hard times. Damn hard times. I need people who will stay in this community and keep going. We're in a bit of a boon right now. But we've gone through decades where everyone around here eked out an existence.

They did it, and I helped where I could. This land is hard. The work is hard. The people are harder. They stick. That's the type of people I need and want in my town. Phil and Sarah are that type of people. If you're kin to Phil, I have a feeling you're that type of people, too. I'm willing to take a chance on you if you're willing to take a chance on Hollister. But I don't need you folding at the first sign of trouble."

Kayla sat back and looked at the man across from her. "Sir, I've never walked away from hardships. This town and the people in it are tough. I'm made of the same material. I won't disappoint you."

Senior extended his hand, and Kayla put her hand in his. "Kayla Bryce, you'll have your store. We break ground in the spring."

"Mr. Hollister, you have yourself a clothier, seamstress, and quilter. I still don't dance."

Senior barked out a laugh. "Welcome home, Miss Bryce. Welcome home."

CHAPTER 21

Alex tugged at his suit. He'd put on weight since moving to Hollister. Most of it was in his chest and arms. The suit jacket was tight, but it would have to do. He slipped into his dress shoes and grabbed his keys before checking to ensure everything was ready. Kayla was spending the night tonight. Granted, they'd had a few after-work interludes, so it wasn't like they hadn't had sex since they'd returned from Rapid. But he wanted to sleep with her in his arms and wake up with her beside him.

He rolled his eyes. *Caveman mentality much, Thompson?* Maybe, but there was something about Kayla. She brought out his protective impulses. Not that she needed him to protect her. She was a completely capable adult. But when he was with her, or thinking about her, or hell, breathing, his instinct was to keep her from harm. Protect her from not only the unknown in the world but the fears and disappointments that life served.

He stopped before he reached for the door and pulled his phone from his inside breast pocket. He flipped through his contacts and hit up Ian Ridgeway. It was a good thing he ran into the man and visited with him during the debacle of a storm when he was trying to get out of Atlanta. Thank God he had the foresight to get the man's number. Ian was the only person he knew who was currently in California.

>> Hey, were you able to get the candies?

>>> Sure was. Had to get some for myself. Damn good. Box is supposed to be there three days before Christmas.

>> Thanks for the assist, man. Online delivery couldn't get it here in time.

>>>No worries. You owe me one.

>> Any time.

He'd had to call Nail and see if he could remember the name of the candy that Kayla loved. He knew it started with an S. Between the two of them and an internet search, they found the one she'd mentioned. He hoped.

He got into the truck he'd borrowed from Nail and drove the short distance to Phil and Sarah's house. He chuckled as he wiped his sweaty hand on his slacks. Why in the hell did he feel like a kid on prom night?

He parked the truck, kept it running, and walked to the door. It opened before he knocked. Phil, in a suit, greeted him at the door. "Dang, that's handy work," Alex said as he motioned toward the suit adjusted for his cast.

"Kayla." Phil chuckled. "I was just going to wear a shirt and jeans, but she had other ideas. The ladies are putting on the finishing touches. Come on in."

"Wow, Alex. Nice suit," Kimber said from the front room.

"When did you get old enough to have kids?" Alex asked her as he walked in.

"Ha, don't even suggest it for another twenty or thirty years," Phil growled.

Kimber rolled her eyes. "This is Scott, and this is Jared. They're Declan and Melody's babies. Carol and I are watching them tonight along with Cody."

"I don't need a babysitter," Cody said from in front of the television.

"I know, dude, but you're going to help us with Jared and Scott, right?" Kimber said from the floor where she was playing with the boys.

"Sure." Cody slumped off the couch and flopped onto his belly on the floor. He pushed a brightly colored car toward Jared, and the little guy crawled after it.

Kimber looked up and winked at her dad. Alex could see the pride on his face. He and Sarah had raised good kids.

Sarah stepped into the front room. "Wow. Honey, you look amazing." Sarah was wearing a red dress and had her hair swept up.

"Momma, you look beautiful." Carol stood from where she was playing with Scott. "Is that a new dress?"

"No, it isn't." Phil's smile said more than his words could. "But she looks more beautiful in it now than ever." He walked over and kissed his wife, who was blushing.

"Thank you." She slid her arm down Phil's suit. "You look fabulous."

"I clean up well," Phil agreed, and they both laughed. But Alex wasn't looking at Phil. He was staring at the woman in the doorway. By God, he knew she was beautiful. He'd held her naked body against him, but the dress she wore was magnificent.

"Beautiful." Alex found the word and walked toward Kayla. He took her hand and spun her. The black dress fit her perfectly, molding to her curves and hinting at the beauty underneath. "Absolutely beautiful." He'd never seen her in makeup. She didn't need it, but tonight she wore it, and the total effect was mind-blowing. He leaned down and kissed her. When he lifted, she smiled shyly.

"It isn't too much?"

"No. You look perfect. I'm going to be the proudest man at that dance."

"Speak for yourself, young man." Phil put his good arm around his wife. "I think most of the men tonight would say those are fighting words."

Alex chuckled. "No offense meant."

"None taken." Sarah laughed. "Shall we go?"

"Coat?" Alex asked and looked around.

"I'm afraid it's the puffy white coat for me. I don't have a dress coat." Kayla grabbed the coat off the hook by the door. Alex helped her into hers and made sure Phil had Sarah's coat managed before he opened the door.

Sarah paused and asked, "Girls, do you need anything before we go?"

"Nope. We've got this," Kimber said. "Go have fun. Don't stay out too late."

Carol laughed. "Yeah, or you'll get grounded."

Phil groaned. "I've raised monsters."

Kayla laughed. "You've raised strong daughters. Night, girls."

"Night!" The echoes followed the four of them out the door. Kayla was very careful to watch where she stepped, as was Sarah. Alex held her hand and opened the door for her, then helped her into the truck. He didn't wait for Phil and Sarah. They could manage. Besides, he wanted to get to the community hall, find a dark corner to park in, and get a taste of the angel in the truck next to him.

"You look very nice, too. I'm not sure I said that. I thought it about a thousand times." Kayla laughed.

"That dress is killer on you. A perfect ten." Alex reached over and held her hand. "I'm the luckiest man in the state."

"And I'm the luckiest woman." She sighed, and the smile that was across her face was radiant. "I get to stay in Hollister."

"It was an amazing day all around. Look." He pulled onto what the townspeople called the main street. The candy canes lit up and tracked your eye to the Christmas tree with the star on top.

"Oh, wow. That's beautiful."

They drove down the street. "Oh, look. The medical building is decorated, too. Gen's diner has lights, and look at Sandersons' grocery. We need to decorate Uncle Phil's garage." She laughed. "I love Christmas. I love how humanity seems to mellow and people are less consumed with their own lives."

"The season does seem to bring out the best in people." Alex crossed the highway and found a parking spot in the almost full lot behind the Bit and Spur. He didn't turn off the truck but killed the lights. "How about we have a proper hello?" He leaned over, and she came to him without hesitation. That time, he kissed her how he wanted to when he first saw her. With the possessiveness and need that their random moments together had stoked throughout the week.

He broke the kiss when he needed oxygen, which was the only reason he moved away from her. "Do we have to go in?" Alex put his forehead on hers.

"Probably." She breathed out softly. "We don't have to stay long, though."

Alex kissed her forehead. "Let's go. I'll show off the most beautiful woman in the territory."

Kayla kissed him again. "I'm not beautiful."

He took her chin between his finger and thumb. "To me, you are beyond beautiful."

She stared at him for a moment. "And you're the most handsome man I've ever seen."

He studied her for a moment longer. "I know this, between us, is red hot and new. I want this to be exclusive."

Kayla blinked. "Um … I thought we were dating?"

"Yes, exclusively."

She made a face. "I always assumed dating and exclusive went hand in hand."

Alex shook his head. "You'd be surprised."

"Probably. I'm not seeing anyone else, Alex. I'm not built like that."

"Neither am I. I just wanted it stated." Because he'd seen some ugly stuff happen to men who made assumptions.

"Then it's stated." She kissed him again. "Let's go, so we can leave."

He laughed and turned off the truck. He helped her out of the truck and through the parking lot. It looked like Declan had cleared the lot for the occasion. No snow or ice to be found. They went into the hall and checked Kayla's coat. He kept the ticket. The profit from the coat closet would be split between the two churches, or so the sign at the entrance of the building said.

They went through the main double doors. Alex was right. The entire town and most of the ranchers in the area were in attendance. Clothing ranged from new jeans and shiny cowboy boots to suits and cocktail dresses. There was music playing in the background and a stage with a drum set, guitars, and an electric piano on the stage. There were Edison lightbulbs strung from the rafters of the vast hall. Twinkle lights adorned two massive Christmas trees that flanked the stage.

He guided Kayla through the crowd, and they said hello to people they knew. When they hit the dance floor, he took her into his arms. "I can't move like I used to, but I think I can manage a slow dance."

Kayla laid her head on his shoulder, and they danced to the music. The song transitioned, and they kept dancing. She looked up at him finally. "I'm staying in Hollister." She'd struggled to get around that idea since she'd told him about what Senior had offered her. It wasn't how she'd pictured her life, what she thought she wanted. Thank God. It was so much more.

"Yes. *We* are staying in Hollister." Alex stared down at her. "We're staying."

She smiled. "Living here won't be easy."

Alex shrugged. "Life is hard. The location doesn't make it any easier or harder. I think everyone has the capacity to stand strong, but few have the inclination. The people here do."

She nodded and glanced around the packed dance floor. "I told Senior I thought of Hollister as home."

Alex glanced at the people. Surprisingly, he knew quite a few. "So do I." He shook his head. "Two months ago, I wouldn't have. But this place …"

"It's special," Kayla finished as they swayed to the music.

"It has special people," Alex said and dropped a kiss on her lips.

When he lifted, she smiled up at him. "Special people who mean the world to me."

Alex nodded. "Your family."

"And you." She looked down for a moment before she lifted her gaze. "You have to know I'm hooked on you."

Alex pressed her closer to him. "I'm glad because you mean the world to me. I couldn't imagine my day without you in it. I don't want to imagine the nights, but ..."

"It would be way too fast to move in with you," she finished his sentence and then added, "I mean, what would people think?"

"That we'd never last. That I'm taking advantage of you. Your uncle Phil should fire me." Alex rattled off all the reasons he'd thought of each time he wanted to ask her to just stay with him.

"Or that I'm easy. That I don't have any sense hooking up with someone I've only known for a short time. I'm just looking for someone to take care of me," she added.

"Or that we're adults and we know our own mind. Time be damned." Alex looked down at her.

"We do know our own minds." She bit her

bottom lip. "I know I want to talk with you, and you're not there. I know I don't want to sleep alone. I know it's crazy fast, but I can't help thinking that it is crazy perfect, too."

"Crazy perfect. God, that's exactly how I'd describe it. You literally hit me over the head, and I haven't been able to get you out of my mind since."

She giggled and leaned forward, stage-whispering, "Yah, well, I landed on my ass when I met you, so I know what you mean."

Alex barked out a laugh and spun Kayla. Twirling her back into him, he clenched her against his chest. "So, when are you going to move in with me?"

"After Christmas. New Year's." She swayed with him.

"And your aunt and uncle?"

"No, they can stay at their house."

Alex laughed again. He always seemed to laugh when Kayla was around. Her inner beauty, unexpected snark, and the goodness in her heart had snared him in a trap he had no desire to release. She filled his life. He put his chin on top of her head, and they danced. She filled his life. The enormity of that statement sunk in as the song changed to something faster. He led her off the dance floor.

"Kayla, Alex, here, we have room," Gen Wheeler said.

They took a seat at the table. Alex shook Andrew Wheeler's hand. "We saved the table, but everyone is still dancing." Gen shrugged.

"Why aren't you?" Kayla asked.

"Ah, well, my stomach's been off today. Twirling around like that would not be a good thing." Gen smiled at Andrew, and he put his arm around her.

"I'd rather not dance, anyway." Andrew turned to him. "I heard you were in the Army. I was in the Marines. RECON."

Alex lifted his eyebrows. "Knew a couple of guys on a RECON team. We worked with them on a couple of missions in the sandbox."

Andrew turned to him as the women talked. "We?"

"1SFOD." If Andrew knew, then he'd understand the designation. If he didn't, it was easy to explain away.

Andrew leaned forward. "Why are you working as a mechanic?"

"Wrecked my leg in training. They medically discharged me."

Andrew made a noise. "Me, too. Someday,

when you want to swap stories, we'll have a beer or two."

"I'll swap stories, but two drinks would put me under the table."

Andrew smiled. "Army slackers."

"Marine jarheads," Alex returned.

Andrew stuck out his hand again. "Welcome to Hollister. I hope you stick around."

Alex glanced over at Kayla. "I plan on it."

CHAPTER 22

Kayla slipped into the truck Alex had started and warmed up before returning to get her. "Thank you for tonight." Kayla sighed. "I had such a good time."

They'd stayed until the band stopped playing. The older people had drifted away, but five tables of younger couples stayed to visit. Kayla and Alex met so many people from neighboring ranches. The Marshall ranch and the Hollister ranch were well represented. Declan brought in a crock pot of hot apple cider and a small bottle of Fireball, along with some Styrofoam cups. There were no takers for the whiskey, but the crock pot was empty by the time Alex went with the other men to start up the vehicles.

"This place keeps surprising me." Alex shook his head. "I had a great time, and when I walked in there, I was sure it would be a drudgery to endure."

Kayla turned in her seat to look at him. "Did you? Why?"

He shrugged. "I really couldn't tell you. I just figured it would be one of those things. In the military, we called it mandatory fun. You know, show up, be seen, then leave."

"Well, did you have fun? Mandatorily or otherwise?"

"I did. As I said, this town keeps surprising me."

"I noticed you didn't accept the invite out to the Hollisters' tomorrow."

Alex stopped at the stop sign. "I'm trying." He drove through the intersection and entered the parking area for the cabins.

Kayla put her hand on his arm. "Alex, I wasn't being derogatory. I thought it was because you wanted to spend the day with me."

He pulled into his parking spot and turned off the motor. Turning to her, he took her hand. "I want to spend more than tomorrow with you."

She stared at him for a moment. There was something in his tone. Something she felt in her soul. "I feel the same way."

He kissed her lightly and then got out, coming to her side of the truck to open the door. "Nope, you'll ruin your shoes." He picked her up from the seat and hip-checked the door, closing it after them. Then he walked slowly to the steps and put her on the cleared wood. She held his hand as they entered the cabin. He flicked on the light, and she smiled. A trail of petals led to the hallway.

"What is all of this?"

"You'll see." He helped her take off her coat. Taking her hand, he led her down the hall. Kayla peeked around him when he stopped. "Champagne?" Two delicate glasses and a green bottle in an ice bucket sat on top of a small table. "Why?"

"Congratulations on making your dream come true." As he bent down and kissed her, Kayla folded into him. Her body shivered, but not from the winter cold.

He lifted away. "I don't want to ruin that dress. I want you so bad. I might not be as careful as I need to be."

Kayla stepped away from him and lifted the dress over her head. She extended her arm and dropped the thing in the room's corner. She wore a black lace bra, matching panties, and a garter that hooked to her stockings. With the strappy sandals, she hoped she looked enticing and not like a fool. "Fuck me," Alex growled as he stripped off his suit jacket and tore at his tie.

"That's the plan," she said as she walked up to him and put her hands on his. She moved his hands away and slowly unbuttoned his white shirt. Her fingers worked his belt and then slacks. She ran one hand up his chest as the other lowered to circle his cock.

Alex's eyes closed, and his body shuddered under her hands. His hands found her hips, but he did nothing except balance himself. She leaned forward and ran the tip of her tongue around the flat disk of his nipple. God, the noises he made resounded inside her and reverberated with a tenor that caused her sex to clench. She slowly kissed down his chest, dropped to her knees, and pulled his slacks and boxers down farther.

Kayla kissed the tip of Alex's cock. His hands found her hair. He ran his fingers through it but didn't control her actions. She circled the head of his shaft several times before taking him into her mouth. She had little experience pleasing a man like that, but she had an idea of what he wanted. Exploring him with her mouth, she also used her hand to stroke the velvety softness that surrounded his shaft.

He bent down and pulled her up. Confused, she looked at him. "Babe, that was perfect. Better than perfect, but if I didn't stop you, you might have been surprised."

Kayla blinked and then smiled. "You liked it?"

"Oh, yes. I liked it." He bent down to kiss her. She helped him shed his shirt and step out of his slacks as they kissed. He lifted her, and she wrapped her legs around his waist. Alex carefully lowered them to the bed and rose above her. "I'm the luckiest man alive."

His hands traveled down her sides to her waist and the garter belt. He lowered to kiss her and expertly unfastened the closure of her hose. She lifted as he shimmied her panties off her. Their kiss never stopping.

Kayla felt his fingers at the apex of her sex and opened her legs for him. As he lowered to her breasts, his fingers stroked and teased. A tight burning sensation pushed forward and ebbed back. She strained against his fingers, wanting the sensation to come back and stay. Kayla moaned into his mouth.

He lifted and stared down at her as he centered

over her. The feel of his cock as it entered her was good, but she needed ... she needed. "Alex."

"I've got you." He wrapped his arms around her shoulders and filled her. Kayla dug her fingers into his back and lifted her knees, angling her hips to meet his thrust. She closed her eyes. They moved in unison, and that tight, hot, pulsing sensation moved forward again. As it got closer and closer, Alex sped up. She lifted her hips. The trigger to that sensation was just out of her reach. She begged, "More."

Alex's hips snapped forward. Kayla gasped and then bit down on his shoulder as she shattered into grains of sand and floated in the air. She felt Alex climax, but she was lost in the sensation's perfection that was dissipating. The act of sex with Alex transcended the physical. He shattered her on so many levels. The way he cared for her, protected her, valued her. She felt a tear form at the corner of her eye. Alex was so much more than a boyfriend to her. It was as if the universe had put Alex in her path. He was the answer to every question she'd been afraid to ask herself.

He pulled her into him and flicked a blanket that had somehow materialized over them.

"New Year's can't come fast enough," Alex said as he kissed her forehead.

"It scares me, and it thrills me."

"Why does it scare you?"

"What if you figure out you don't like me?"

Alex chuckled. "There's nothing you could do to make that happen."

Kayla bent backward and looked up at him. "I could yank your leg again. The good one this time."

"You wouldn't."

"Yeah, you're right." She settled in next to him. "Alex, I think I'm falling in love with you."

Alex rolled her over, coming on top of her. "Then we're on the same path, babe. Stay with me."

"I promise." Kayla cupped his cheek in her hand. "I'll stay."

CHAPTER 23

Alex watched as the presents were unwrapped. He was enjoying Christmas morning with the Grangers and Kayla. Phil had helped him stage his gifts for Kayla. He wasn't sure if she'd like them, but he hoped she would.

"This is for you." Kayla handed him two boxes. "This one first." She tapped the top box.

He pulled the ribbon holding the box together and took the top off. "What is this?" He held up the material. A flannel-lined mechanic overall in dark blue. Over the right chest, embroidered in gold thread, was his name, Alex 'Bull' Thompson.

"I had to guess the size based on the ones you wore of Uncle Phil's."

"I love them. Thank you." He leaned over to kiss her.

Carol gagged, and Kimber laughed. Kayla turned and looked at her youngest cousin. "Someday, you're not going to think kissing is gag-worthy."

"Yes, I will. Boys are blah. Except you, Daddy, and you, Alex. All the rest are stupid."

"Carol, that wasn't nice," Sarah reprimanded her daughter.

"But it's true." Carol looked at her mom as if the fact that she believed it made it acceptable.

Kayla interrupted, "Open this one."

Alex opened the second box. "An e-reader? Thank you. I just finished the last book I'd brought up here."

"And a gift card." Kimber pointed to it just in case Alex might have missed it.

"And thank you again." He gave Kayla another kiss.

"Now, for Kayla's gift!" Carol clapped her hands and shot up, running to the porch to get coats.

"I have to go outside for my gift?" Kayla looked at him like he was insane.

"Actually, to the shed," Alex said, and both Kimber and Carol laughed and darted out the door with their coats half on and half off. The adults followed at a slower pace.

"Merry Christmas," Alex said and opened the door to the shed, which was actually Phil's private garage.

Kayla stepped in, and Alex moved into the center of the shed and pulled two tarps off of what he'd made.

"Oh my goodness." Kayla moved over, her hand shaking as she touched the smallest quilting frame. "These are perfect."

Kayla turned and launched at him. You'd think he'd be prepared for the tackle hugs, but it almost sat him on his ass. He laughed as he balanced both of them. "You like them?"

"Yes! This will make the classes and my work so much easier. You have them in three sizes!"

"And they all extend and contract, so you'll have whatever size you need." Phil demonstrated. "He thought of everything."

"Did you make them?"

"I did. I pulled the plans off the internet, and Phil helped me hide them in the garage. I worked on them as I could."

"They're perfect. Thank you!"

"I have one more gift for you." Alex walked over

to the last frame and picked up a box wrapped in gold foil with a gold bow.

"This isn't?" She looked at him. "You didn't!"

She pulled the elastic band of the bow off and opened the top of the box. "See's Candies!"

"You said you and your mom had them for special occasions. I thought we could continue the tradition. Christmas is special."

She slapped the lid down on the candy and launched at him again. That time, he caught her.

* * *

"Tell me again why we're talking so damn early?"

Alex laughed at Nail. "I'm bored, and Kayla's probably still asleep, and I know you go into the shop early."

He winced as he shifted. Ken Zorn had called him out to tow an abandoned truck partially obstructing the highway. Alex had left his warm bed and Kayla way too early, but as Phil's cast didn't come off until next week, he was the designated tow truck operator. He'd delivered the abandoned truck to the joint-jurisdiction impound lot in Belle Fourche and was on his way back to Hollister.

"So, stop diverting the question. Are you going to come up for the dance?"

"I'm pretty busy."

Alex snorted. "I don't know, man. Sounds like excuses to me."

"Not really. I'm busy, you know," Nail hedged.

"Tank's back, and you said he was back to work full time. We're inviting you up. There's a spare room." Kayla had moved in on January first. Alex couldn't have been happier. His schedule hadn't really changed. Except for nightly sex, and for that, he'd adapt and overcome.

"Man, she probably doesn't even remember me."

"Dude, there's a Valentine's Day dance. You need to come up on Saturday morning. It'll be worth your time. Allison isn't seeing anyone. Kayla confirmed it."

Nail swore. "You told Kayla?"

"What? No, man. I just listened. Kayla tells me everything she hears at her Thursday night quilting class."

"Ah, fuck. Bull, I got to go. Someone's broken into the shop. The back door is wide open."

"Call me and be careful." Alex hung up. Son of a

bitch. His friend worked way too hard to have that shit happen to him.

Alex drove at a steady clip, heading back to Hollister and glancing at the clock on the dashboard, willing Nail to call him back. He was about thirty miles south of Hollister when a truck passed him.

Alex glanced at it and then did a double-take. "Fuckers."

He grabbed his phone and pushed on the accelerator. "Zorn."

"I'm following a truck with a custom laid down in the back. I think it's a bike from Nail's shop. He got hit last night." He was on the truck's ass, but the fucker must have noticed. He sped up.

"Where are you?"

"Heading north about twenty-five miles from Hollister." Alex gained on the truck again. Only that time, the guy didn't speed up. He brake checked, and Alex tagged the rear bumper. The guy floored it, and Alex did, too. A man leaned out of the passenger side window.

Alex swerved, slamming his foot on the accelerator. He didn't have to see the gun to know the man had one. The truck's windshield shattered, and Alex felt the collision. He jammed on the brakes and worked like hell to control the vehicle as it skidded from the road to the ditch. Alex lost his seat belt and was out of the truck, down behind the wheel as soon as the vehicle lurched to a stop. The pickup had landed nose-down in the ditch. Alex moved carefully, keeping under cover. Fuck, he wished he had a gun. One man pulled another from the cab of the truck. Alex half limped, half jogged to the back of the truck, and flicked the tarp up. The son of a bitch.

He ducked down when he heard the other man coming back to the truck. Alex circled the vehicle, keeping metal between him and the thief as he heard the man thrashing through the cab of the truck. "Where's the fucking gun?"

Alex lifted and peeked into the cab. It was on the passenger side floorboard. Alex moved into the man's line of sight. "Over here, fucktard."

The man lifted and then lunged. Alex was ready. He opened the door and grabbed the gun, tossing it about twenty yards away into the snow. He didn't need a gunfight. Ken was on his way.

"You," the man hissed as he rounded the vehicle's cab. *Oh, the gas dude*.

"Steal any good customs lately, bitch," Alex taunted the man.

"You don't know who you're messing with."

"Oh, I do. A petty thief. That's my bike, motherfucker. My friend built it for me."

A sneer crossed the man's face. "Tough shit."

The thin wail of a siren snapped the man's head to the north. Alex launched, taking out the guy's knees. They landed in the snow together. Alex couldn't let the bastard get up. His leg wouldn't match the man's speed.

The man kicked Alex in the face separating them, but Alex grabbed his boot and pulled, bringing the guy back down to the ground. Alex held onto the foot and rolled onto his back, forcing the man to his stomach. Alex kept the pressure on the thief's foot and climbed onto his back. The fucker grabbed a rock and twisted. His intended target was Alex's head, but Alex moved, and the rock slammed onto his shoulder. His entire arm went numb.

Alex spat out a string of obscenities and pushed the man's face into the snow with his body. "I don't want to kill you, motherfucker. Stop struggling!" Alex adjusted and could grab the man's arm. He let go of the boot and yanked the arm back, putting stress on the shoulder joint. He let go of the man's head and leaned back. His leg may have been a detriment, but he'd bested the fucker.

Ken's patrol vehicle slid to a stop. "Alex!"

"Here!" he called from behind the truck.

"Fuck, you're bleeding."

"I am?" He moved, and Ken handcuffed the son of a bitch. Alex looked down at his shoulder. The guy had opened him up with that rock. His arm wasn't numb, but it felt like a thousand needles were poking him. A hell of a stinger.

"There's another guy. He pulled him out of the truck after the wreck. I threw the gun about twenty yards that way."

"Gun?" Ken's hand went to his weapon, the strap off it in an instant.

"He shot out my windshield." Alex pointed to the tow truck.

"Son of a bitch," Ken spat the words. "Are you okay here while I check on that guy?"

"No problem, go." Alex tried to get up when Ken sprinted to the other man, but his leg gave out. He half crawled, half pushed himself to the truck and used the open passenger door to hold his weight as he lifted himself up. Finally, on his feet, he tried to put weight on his leg. White hot lightning zapped through his leg. Shit, he'd felt that pain before. Fuck, he'd moved in ways he shouldn't have, but damn it, he couldn't let the guy get away.

Ken was on the phone over by the other guy. The thief he'd tackled was trying to get to his knees. "You think you're going somewhere?" Alex said from behind him. He limped forward, braced himself against the truck, and used his good leg to kick the man in the ass, causing the guy to face-plant in the snow. "Stay down." Alex groaned the words. He glanced over at Phil's truck. The bullet hole and web of cracks were too damn close to where he'd been driving.

He wiped at his brow. He was sweating, and it was colder than a witch's tit in a brass bra. The effect of adrenaline. He'd dealt with the aftereffects of the rush before. He drew in a deep breath. If that shot had been over six inches, he might not be there.

His mind flashed to Kayla asleep in their bed. Fuck what people thought. Fuck moving too fast. He was going to make her his. They were destined to be together. He firmly believed that now.

"Hey."

He blinked and looked at Ken. "Are you okay?"

"Nope. Fucked up my leg, and he did a number on my shoulder with that rock. I think I can get

Phil's truck out of the ditch. The back wheels are still on the blacktop. I don't know which one shot at me, but it caused the accident. The windshield shattered, and I couldn't see. We collided. I saw this waste of sperm dragging the other guy out of the truck. Is he okay?"

"Big bump on the head, but he's conscious. Zeke is on his way." Ken nodded to the truck. "How did you know the motorcycle was stolen?"

"The paint job. It's the bike Nail has been building for me. That patch, it's from our old unit. He'd discovered his shop broken into this morning when I was talking to him. About an hour ago."

"Wait, you're Delta Force?" Ken's voice rose. The dirtbag on the ground jerked his head around to look at Alex. Alex groaned and shifted his weight. "I'd appreciate us keeping that quiet."

Ken nodded. "Roger that. Can do."

Alex leaned against the truck and looked at the bike. The scratches in the paint and the chrome were horrible. Fuck, all that work that Nail had done was for nothing. But the patch was plainly visible. "How did you recognize the patch?"

Ken smiled. "You don't play video games, do you?"

Alex frowned. "No."

"Ah, well, some of us do. There's a game, and the character sports that patch."

Zeke's truck pulled along the side of the road. "Where do I go first?"

"Him." Alex pointed to the handcuffed guy sitting on the snowbank, and Ken pointed to Alex.

Zeke shook his head. "Alex?"

"I'll survive. He's got a head injury. Triage." Alex looked at Ken.

"He'll survive, too," Ken defended his decision.

Zeke jogged toward the head injury.

A highway patrol vehicle, lights blazing, pulled alongside Ken's vehicle. Alex squinted to see the trooper as he came into sight. Oh, man … not he … she.

"Trooper Samantha Quinn. This is my new territory. Are you Deputy Ken Zorn?"

Ken nodded. "I am. We have a bit of a situation."

"I can see." The woman looked up at the tow truck. "Bullet hole?"

"Just going to find it," Ken said. "Our tow truck driver tossed it before he took this guy down."

The woman looked at Alex. "Smart man. Most would have tried to play cop and hold the guy with the gun. Never a good idea."

"I'm not a cop, and I know my limitations." Alex

moved on his leg and winced. "I knew I could tackle him, but if he got up, I wouldn't be able to run after him. So, he didn't get up."

The woman nodded. When she turned to Ken, Alex saw the color of her hair. It was dark red and pulled to the base of her neck in a tight bun. "Your crime scene, Deputy. Can I help, or do you want me to roll?"

"I'll take all the help I can get." Ken nodded toward where the gun landed. "Bag and tag the gun. His prints are on it. He threw it. Any other prints would probably be our shooters."

"I got it. Let me grab my crime scene kit." She jogged back to her vehicle.

"Nice," Alex said.

"What?" Ken looked back at him.

"It was nice of her to offer to help."

Ken nodded, still looking at the trooper. "Damn nice."

Zeke brought the man with the cut on his forehead over. It was bandaged. "He'll be okay to transport. No apparent concussion, but you'll need him looked at once you get him down south."

"Thanks, Doc. I'll be back for that one." Ken marched the man up the embankment. He talked with the trooper and then put the man in the back of her patrol car. Ken leaned in and spoke to the guy as the trooper watched.

"So, let me look at that shoulder." Obviously, Zeke wasn't interested in what was going on.

"A cut and a stinger. Numbed me right out. Then when I got feeling back, it was a million needles sticking me at the same time."

"Mmmmm …" Zeke made a noncommittal noise.

"Leg?" he asked as he poked around the jagged cut the rock had caused.

"It is not happy with me."

"Anything more than that?"

"Don't think so. Feels like what it did when I didn't follow the PT's instructions and pushed too hard."

Zeke nodded. "That cut needs to be cleaned out, and you'll need a tetanus shot if you haven't had one lately. There's some metal lodged in that rock."

"Nah. I'm up to date." He'd just gotten out of the military. Hell, he had every shot known to man and some that most people would never have to get.

"All right. You can ride in with me."

"No, sir. I'm taking the truck in. I need to explain to Phil what happened."

Zeke glanced at the shattered window of the tow truck. "You can't drive that."

He turned to the doctor and smiled. It wasn't a pleasant thing. "Watch me."

* * *

A KNOCK at the exam room door brought Zeke around. "Hey, Billy. What's up?"

Billy walked into the room. "Heard Alex had a tussle with some bad guys. I was in town and thought I'd check in. Can I talk to him for a minute?"

"Sure. I'm done." Zeke turned back to him. "Put these in your coat pocket. You can shower. If the bandage peels away, just slap a couple of these on." The cut wasn't too deep, but the blow from the rock would leave a hell of a bruise on his shoulder. It was already black and purple.

Billy waited for the doctor to leave and shut the door. "You going to live?"

"I will." Alex moved and groaned. "I've been hurt worse. Why are you here?"

Billy snorted. "Love the direct approach. You've

been studying the courses, and you know the layout of the training facility."

Alex nodded. "I've got it down. Why? You leaving?"

"Don't know. Isaac is on a mission, and I'm on standby. That's why I came to town. Heard about the excitement and waited around to see you. I saw Phil leave and figured I had a few minutes before your woman showed up. Anyway, we have two marksmen in training. Both are okay. You were a hundred times better. They're trying, though. I'll give them credit. I'm putting you on notice. They'll eat up the rounds and practice, but you may have to do some instruction on an evening or weekend day. Just to keep them focused and on target."

"I can do that. Thank you for giving me the heads up."

Billy shrugged. "I read your profile. You don't like surprises. I get that."

Alex dropped his head and blinked at Billy. "My profile?"

"I told you, Guardian knows everything about you. Even where your momma is, if you ever want that information."

Alex stared at the man, who was supposed to be dead. "No. I have zero interest in finding or talking to her. She made her choices, and they didn't involve me."

Billy nodded, and a smile spread across his face. Alex rolled his eyes. "That was a test, wasn't it?"

"Good to know you don't hold a grudge, newb." Billy held up his hand. "I know, I know. It's just fun to rattle your cage. Take care, Alex. I'll let you know about my mission as soon as I know."

"Thanks, Billy," Alex said as the man left.

He rolled his shoulders and glanced at the clock on the wall. Damn it, what a day, and it had just begun.

CHAPTER 24

Kayla sat beside Alex, holding his hand. When Phil had stopped by the cabin and told her what had happened, she'd been in shock, almost in denial. Not there in the diner, though. Not when she was looking at his torn shirt and seeing how stiff he was. The bullet hole in the windshield of Uncle Phil's tow truck could have killed Alex.

"Hey, are you okay?" Alex whispered as everyone around them talked about this morning's excitement.

"No. They could have killed you."

"They didn't. I'm okay."

She shook her head sharply and whispered, "That doesn't help how I'm feeling."

Alex dropped his chin on top of her head. He had to be exhausted. "What are you feeling?"

Her insides were liquid, fear boiled just under her skin, and she wanted to scream, to cry, to point at the windshield and demand someone make the person responsible for it pay. She drew a shaky breath. "Terrified. I could have lost you."

"I feel the same way. I don't want to lose you. Ever."

She leaned into him. "Ever."

"Is that the new trooper?" Edna asked as Ken's vehicle carrying one suspect and the new trooper's car carrying the other stopped outside the diner.

Allison, Ciera, Stephanie, and Gen moved over to get a better look. Kayla didn't need to. The woman officer was striking. Tall. She didn't smile, but that didn't matter. She was beautiful.

Ken jogged to the diner and opened the door. "Alex, I'll be back for your statement. We're taking these two down and booking them." Alex nodded, then Ken shut the door and jogged back to his SUV. The trooper got in and took off first, and Ken followed her.

Phil and Sarah sat across from them. "I'll pay for the replacement of the windshield." Alex stopped apologizing for the damage to the tow truck because Phil said he'd fire him if he didn't.

"You will not. I have insurance, and that's what it's for." Phil harrumphed a bit. "I'm just damn glad you're going to be okay."

"I don't know. Zeke about killed me cleaning out that cut."

"Can you whine any louder there, Alex?" Zeke said from his seat, where he was eating with his wife.

"I'm sure I could if I tried."

"Go home today. Warm soak that leg. Don't let it get too stiff. Keep moving."

Alex rolled his eyes. "I know the drill. I can take care of myself."

"Says the man who was shot at and took down two thieves," Edna said from her table. Her ladies nodded their heads. "That was brave, Alex. What made you do it?"

Kayla wanted to know that, too.

"It wasn't an act of heroics. I knew they'd a stolen bike in the back. They brake-checked me. Obviously, they didn't know a truck that size can't stop on a dime."

"That's the truth," Phil agreed.

"I tapped the back of the truck. Probably didn't

even dent the bumper. They sped up, and the next thing I knew, a gun was pointing my way. Instinct kicked in." He shrugged.

"Instinct?" Stephanie asked from her table. "You're used to having people shoot at you?"

"No, ma'am, but I'm prior military, and we trained for all types of contingencies. That was the instinct I was talking about."

Kayla watched as people nodded. "When we both ended up on the side of the road, I knew I had to get out of the tow truck fast. I think dropping down was what jarred my leg, but adrenaline kept me moving even when I shouldn't have moved."

Zeke nodded. "Probably."

"I was glad Ken showed up when he did. Then the new trooper came on scene right after Zeke pulled up. End of story." Alex took a drink of his coffee and adjusted. She saw the wince.

"What happened to the truck and the stolen motorcycle?" Gen asked from behind the counter.

"The trooper called up someone from Belle to fetch them," Phil spoke for Alex. "Alex waited at the scene to see if they needed any help before he brought the rig home."

"And I'll pay for that windshield."

Phil growled. "Insurance will pay for the windshield. You did what any one of us would do if we were in your place."

Edna snorted. "Sorry, not me. I'm not that adventurous."

"Says the woman who takes pictures of Bigfoot." Ciera chuckled as she refilled coffee cups.

"Well, we're not sure it is a Bigfoot." Edna sighed. "I looked at the negative. It was scratched right where the thing I thought was a Bigfoot was." She shrugged. "Not in the exact shape, but it makes me doubt whether it is a Bigfoot, you know?"

The café quieted. "When did you figure that out, Edna?" Belinda asked.

"Oh, I was talking to Mr. Marshall, and I showed him the photo. He asked to see the negative, and what do you know, scratched. I should have thought to look at the negative sooner." She shrugged. "The mysteries of the world should remain that, I guess."

"Except UFOs," Doris Altham said.

"Right. Because those are real," Edna agreed.

Kayla smiled at the women before turning to Alex. "How about I take you back to the cabin so you can get cleaned up?"

"Thankfully, the inquisition is over. No one

should stop by to bother you. Told you this was the best way to disseminate the news," Phil whispered.

"Ken will stop by, but if he's just heading down now, it won't be until much later tonight." Sarah looked at Alex. "If you need anything, you two let us know. We've got odds and ends from countless accidents and broken bones."

Alex smiled. "Thank you, Sarah, but what I need is a shower and to stretch out for a bit. I can't stay still, so I'll do some of the exercises my PT showed me. I've tweaked my leg before. It will be fine in a couple of days."

"Then, no work tomorrow," Phil said and held up a hand. "No argument. We're caught up, and I can manage by myself."

"Honestly, it would be better if I moved on it. I'll let you know if I need to stop. I won't risk screwing my leg up permanently."

"We'll see. I'll stop by in the morning on the way to work. Sleep in, at least."

"We can do that." Kayla placed her hand carefully on Alex's leg. "Ready?"

"I am." She slid out of the booth and waited as he made the move to get over and off the bench seat. He planted a hand on the table and one on the back of the booth and lifted himself into a standing position. His face broke out in a sweat, and he paled. "I remember this feeling." He dropped his arm around her shoulder, and she let him use her as a crutch. Gen opened the door, and they made their way out to a chorus of goodbyes and feel betters. Kayla helped him lower into her crossover and drove them back to the cabin. She helped him out of the small SUV, and they single-stepped up the stairs.

"What do you need?" she asked as soon as they got into the cabin.

"Help me get undressed. I need to soak in a warm shower, then stretch out and rest for a bit."

She helped him down the hall and out of his clothes. The cut on his shoulder was bandaged. "How are you going to shower and not get that wet?"

"Doc said I could get it wet. There are butterfly bandages in my coat when or if they come off. No stitches." He hissed as he bent so she could take off his boots and jeans.

"Did Zeke give you anything for the pain?"

"One mild painkiller. I'll need it to relax after the shower. After that, I'll take over-the-counter meds." He used her as a crutch to get to the shower.

"What else can I do?" She felt helpless, and she was still scared. Her nerves jangled against each other, keeping her uptight.

"Hey."

She looked up at him.

"I'm okay."

"You could have died." She felt tears fill her eyes.

"Babe." He stroked her cheek with his finger. "You're crying."

"I'm sorry." She wiped at her eyes. "I was so scared when Phil told me what happened. But that bullet hole." She sniffed and wiped at tears again. "I just found you."

"Come in here. I want to hold you."

She stripped out of her clothes and went into his arms. The warm water poured over both of them. "I'm being a fool."

"No, you're not." He leaned against her, and she gladly accepted some of his weight. "After Ken got on scene, it hit me, too. The thought of not seeing you again."

She sniffed and nodded against his chest. "It's so fast. All of this, but the emotions, I swear, they're real."

He stroked her back comfortingly. "They are real. We'll be okay. We're together."

Kayla nodded. She closed her eyes and held the man she'd fallen in love with. It was too soon to say the words, but she could show him with her actions, just like he was showing her. She knew he loved her, just as he knew she loved him. The words didn't need to be said. Not yet.

CHAPTER 25

Valentine's Day.

Alex carefully placed the one very special chocolate from Kayla's favorite candy shop on the plate and stood back. The vase he was using he'd borrowed from Sarah. One perfect red rose stood tall in the delicate glass holder. The champagne was chilled, and the glasses were ready.

Sarah had manufactured a reason to call Kayla over that afternoon so he could set up the house. He lit the candles and took a deep breath. His nerves were jumping, and his mouth was as dry as a mud pit in the Sahara Desert.

He heard her crossover pull up and took a

breath. He opened the door, and she jogged in, her head buried in her hood. The snow was blowing sideways, and a storm was raging down on them from the Rockies.

"Whew! It's coming down out there." She spun and took off her coat, facing the door. He took it from her and hung it up, and she smiled up at him. "Sarah is a lost cause with sewing. I told her I'd just take care of everything from now on." She wrapped her arms around his neck and toed up. He kissed her until they were both breathless. She slipped down on her heels and sighed. "The way you kiss me."

"The way you kiss me back." He tightened his hold as she leaned against him. Still not looking past him. *He was going to have an aneurysm. Straight up. His blood pressure had to be a thousand over five hundred. How could she not hear his heart pounding?*

She finally pulled out of the hug and turned around. "What?" She took in everything. "For me?"

"For you." He took her hand and walked her to the counter where they ate. He poured each of them a glass of champagne. "You're drinking?" Her eyes were wide.

"Today, I am." He took a sip of the champagne,

but it did nothing to ease the dryness of his mouth and throat.

"Is this ..." She picked up the chocolate.

"It is." A very special candy that he'd called a favor in to have made.

"It's big!"

"Handmade, special request. Valentine's Day, you know."

She took a sip of her champagne. "Maybe I should save it for tonight. We could share it."

"Kayla, eat the candy. Please, for me?" Before he lost his ever-loving mind.

"Are you sure? Here, you have the first bite." She held it up to him. He closed his mouth and shook his head. "I got it for you. Just you."

Her smile faltered for a moment. "Are you sure?"

"Positive." *Trust me. Please eat the candy.* He begged her silently.

"Okay." She lifted it to her lips and carefully broke through the chocolate shell. The ring he'd purchased for her dropped, but she caught it. Her mouth was full of chocolate, a diamond ring in one hand and a chocolate shell in the other. She screamed something, but for the love of God, he couldn't understand what she'd said.

Kayla tossed the chocolate on the plate and chewed as quickly as she could. "Oh my God! Is this?" She looked at him and then at the ring. He took it from her and slid it on her left finger. With extreme care, he dropped to one knee. He'd worked hard to make sure he could do it by today.

"Kayla Marie Bryce, I love you. I know this is fast, but I don't care. Will you marry me?"

She dropped to her knees in front of him. "You've never said it before."

"Yet we both know it, don't we?"

"Yes. I love you. I will marry you." She wrapped her arms around him, and he kissed her on the floor of that little cabin during a snowstorm in South Dakota. He held her close and thanked God and the universe for Hollister and for Blessing's encouragement. He'd taken her advice and found a home. A Home for Love.

THE END

TO READ the other Season Three Long Road Home Series, Click here:

MARYANN JORDAN'S THINKING OF HOME
ABBIE ZANDER'S TOO CLOSE TO HOME
CAT JOHNSON'S HOMECOMING
CAITLYN O'LEARY HOME AT LAST

Are you interested in reading Ken's story? Click here.

ALSO BY KRIS MICHAELS

Kings of the Guardian Series

Jacob: Kings of the Guardian Book 1

Joseph: Kings of the Guardian Book 2

Adam: Kings of the Guardian Book 3

Jason: Kings of the Guardian Book 4

Jared: Kings of the Guardian Book 5

Jasmine: Kings of the Guardian Book 6

Chief: The Kings of Guardian Book 7

Jewell: Kings of the Guardian Book 8

Jade: Kings of the Guardian Book 9

Justin: Kings of the Guardian Book 10

Christmas with the Kings

Drake: Kings of the Guardian Book 11

Dixon: Kings of the Guardian Book 12

Passages: The Kings of Guardian Book 13

Promises: The Kings of Guardian Book 14

The Siege: Book One, The Kings of Guardian Book 15

The Siege: Book Two, The Kings of Guardian Book 16

A Backwater Blessing: A Kings of Guardian Crossover

Novella

Montana Guardian: A Kings of Guardian Novella

Guardian Defenders Series

Gabriel

Maliki

John

Jeremiah

Frank

Creed

Sage

Bear

Guardian Security Shadow World

Anubis (Guardian Shadow World Book 1)

Asp (Guardian Shadow World Book 2)

Lycos (Guardian Shadow World Book 3)

Thanatos (Guardian Shadow World Book 4)

Tempest (Guardian Shadow World Book 5)

Smoke (Guardian Shadow World Book 6)

Reaper (Guardian Shadow World Book 7)

Phoenix (Guardian Shadow World Book 8)

Valkyrie (Guardian Shadow World Book 9)

Flack (Guardian Shadow World Book 10)

Ice (Guardian Shadow World Book 11)

Hollister (A Guardian Crossover Series)

Andrew (Hollister-Book 1)

Zeke (Hollister-Book 2)

Declan (Hollister- Book 3)

Ken (Hollister - Book 4)

Hope City

Hope City - Brock

HOPE CITY - Brody- Book 3

Hope City - Ryker - Book 5

Hope City - Killian - Book 8

Hope City - Blayze - Book 10

The Long Road Home

Season One:

My Heart's Home

Season Two:

Searching for Home (A Hollister-Guardian Crossover Novel)

Season Three:

A Home for Love

STAND ALONE NOVELS

A Heart's Desire - Stand Alone

Hot SEAL, Single Malt (SEALs in Paradise)

Hot SEAL, Savannah Nights (SEALs in Paradise)

Hot SEAL, Silent Knight (SEALs in Paradise)

ABOUT THE AUTHOR

Wall Street Journal and USA Today Bestselling Author, Kris Michaels is the alter ego of a happily married wife and mother. She writes romance, usually with characters from military and law enforcement backgrounds.